CHAS WILLIAMSON
Seeking Series: Book Two

SEEKING
Happiness

ISBN 13: 978-1-945670-95-4
ISBN 10: 1-945670-95-9

Year of the Book
135 Glen Avenue
Glen Rock, PA 17327

Dedication

Seeking Happiness is dedicated to the woman of my dreams, the one who turned my head so many years ago. The one who still takes my breath away. You have given me the power, the strength, the drive and the encouragement to become what I am. If not for you, I would still be dreaming instead of seeing my dreams come true. You are my happiness, my love and my life. I look forward to spending eternity with you. I love you forever. Thank you for being the pearl I reached for, for marrying me and making my life complete. I couldn't be me without you!

Acknowledgments

To God, for your abundant blessings and for bringing the shift in our life. Our cup runneth over because of You.

To Janet, for your encouragement, advice, guidance, and most importantly, love.

To my family, for their encouragement and support.

To Travis, for helping with all the techie stuff.

To Sarah, for your medical advice.

To our beta readers – Jackie, Sarah and Janet.

To Demi, for making the entire publishing process enjoyable.

To Laurie, for helping me grow as an author.

*Get exclusive
never-before-published content!*

www.chaswilliamson.com

A Paradise Short Story

Download your free copy of
Skating in Paradise today!

Chapter 1

The salty scent of the blue Pacific waves teased Kelly's mind as the water crested over her feet. The warmth of her husband's hand was a confirmation. This day, this time of life was absolutely perfect. Her baby sister Kaitlin's snowy white wedding dress was a contrast to the black coral sands on the beach at the end of the road to Hana. Love radiated all around her, from the soon to be newlyweds, from her family, and especially from her husband.

Kelly kissed his hand, whispering, "I love you, Ballister." Since they had the same first name, she had always called him by his last name. His shoulder length blond hair and goatee matched the colors of his tropical themed shirt.

Without looking at her, he answered softly, "Pay attention. It's almost over."

The pastor finished the ceremony, proclaiming he was the first to introduce Mr. and Mrs. Jeremy Roberts. Jeremy wrapped his arms around his bride, kissing her deeply.

Kelly hugged herself. *Father, please bless them with happiness, like you did for me.*

***

"Santa come yet?"

"I dunno."

"Let's go see."

"Shhh. It's too dark."

Kelly rolled over in bed, smiling at the conversation between her children in the next room. The majority of the gifts were at home. She brought just a few to keep the magic alive for the rug rats. A slight pounding nagged behind her temples as she snuggled her head deeply into the soft silky pillow. *Too much wine. And dancing. No, never too much dancing. Not enough sleep, yeah that's it.* Kelly instinctively reached for her husband's hand, but found nothing. Squinting in the pre-dawn shadows, his silhouette was perched on the edge of the bed.

"You okay?"

"Another damned headache. A bad one."

"What can I do? Want Tylenol? Maybe more sleep?"

"Forget it. Kids are up. Ready to open gifts."

"Want coffee?"

He nodded before shuffling to the bathroom.

She followed him in, patting his arm. "Don't worry. When we get home, we'll see the doctor."

Ballister was distracted not only during breakfast, but also while their children opened the gifts. Before she could ask if his headache was worse, his cell rang. He slipped out to the lanai, closing the door firmly behind him.

A shiver ran up her spine. He never carried his cell with him and never left the room to take a call.

Kelly Junior, whom mommy called K.J., asked, "Daddy okay?"

An eerie tingling feeling worked its way from her hands to her shoulder. "Sure, sweetie. Daddy had to get the phone, that's all."

A loud scream brought Kelly back to the present. The twins, Tessa and Melinda, were fighting over the same toy. "Girls, girls. Stop it!" She comforted and re-directed her daughters, eliminating the tension between them.

The momentary sound of the surf pounding the shore caught her attention. Looking up, Ballister closed the sliding door behind him. His eyes didn't meet her gaze.

"What's going on?"

"Nothing."

"Who was on the phone?"

"Nobody."

"So nothing's going on and nobody called?"

His eyes suddenly locked on hers as his voice barked, "Leave me alone! Why do you always have to, to... oh just forget it! Leave me the hell alone." He stormed into the bedroom, slamming the door so hard that the pictures on each side of the jamb crashed to the floor.

Davy, the youngest, started bawling from the noise. The tip of Kelly's nose tingled as she fought back tears. Ballister had never treated her like that, especially in front of the children. Her twins clung to her knees. K.J.'s eyes were fearfully wide as he asked, "Is Daddy sick?"

The door stood there like a defiant middle finger sandwiched between the white hotel walls. "Yes. I think Daddy is sick today, very sick."

Chapter 2

H er hands cramped in frustration over Ballister's childish behavior. She'd balled them into fists. He had been too 'sick' to meet with the extended family for lunch. The children were cranky, ready for a nap. *Good. We need a few minutes of alone time to discuss your attitude.* The cramps made it difficult to get the key into the lock. Finally, she swung the door open to discover him sitting on a chair, staring out the window, suitcase by his side.

Kelly's teeth started to hurt. She realized she was clenching her jaws. She forced her muscles to relax. "What's this?"

He didn't even look at her. "Get your parents to watch the kids."

"Why?"

"Just do it, woman."

Her parents arrived within five minutes of the call, taking the children back to their room. Random sharp pains shot through her chest as she tried to understand what was happening. The door had barely closed when Kelly angrily turned toward Ballister. "Explain what the hell is going on."

Ballister walked to the window, staring at the beach as the endless sea rushed to shore. After a few moments, he said, "Kelly, I don't want to do this anymore. Too much of my life is passing me by. There are things I want to do that I just can't do with you being around."

Her mouth was suddenly dry, as her stomach turned. The sensation of being thrown off a tall building came to mind. "What are you talking about?"

He turned to face her. "I don't love you anymore. Haven't for a while. I want out of this sham of a marriage. I'm leaving, for good."

Kelly's breath suddenly refused to enter her lungs. "What?"

Ballister smiled. "Fell out of love with you a while ago." His smile changed to a sneer. "I feel nothing, nothing at all when I hold or kiss you, absolutely nothing. I only feel life is passing me by. So many things I want to do, but you're there, holding me back, every step of the way."

Flashes of light backlit her vision. Anger screamed for a release as she calmly asked, "What exactly am I holding you back from?"

Ballister yawned as he shrugged his shoulders. "Life in general. Look, don't be blonde about it. I found someone else. I'm leaving."

The scent of his aftershave suddenly overwhelmed her senses. She was struggling to keep breakfast down. "What? I gave you everything, everything I had and you want to throw us away? What about our children?"

He shrugged his shoulders again. "Kids always liked you more than me. I'll make this painless. Won't contest anything. You get the kids. My lawyer will file divorce papers January second. My stuff will be gone by the time you get back to L.A. Sell the house to pay off the bills if you want and everything is yours."

Her chin quivered as she fought back tears. Felt like she had been sucker punched. This was no spur of the moment decision. It was pre-meditated.

Kelly's fists again balled as she fought the urge to scream. "So you dump me for someone else and I'm supposed to be fine with that? Who is she?" He laughed in response. "What could she possibly give you I couldn't?"

His smile increased. "Ooh baby. She's been giving me anything and everything I could possibly want, whenever I want." The look on his face as he spewed those words forced bile into her throat.

"Who is she?"

With humor in his eyes, he watched her reaction. "Sherrie. Sherrie Sanford."

The room started to spin. She was the hottest star in Hollywood right now. "The actress?"

"Yep. Emmy-nominated actress, that is. Ms. Sherrie Sanford, my woman, my lover."

The room spun faster. "But she's your patient."

"*Was*. Can't be involved with a patient."

A knock at the door snapped the tension, but Kelly grabbed the arm of the chair to prevent falling over. Her pulse pounded as if it would explode from her veins. "Is that her?"

He shook his head, laughing as he grabbed his suitcase. "I wish! Nope, just my cab." He hoisted his luggage. "Later."

She tried to follow after him, but stumbled. Pain rolled up her knees as they hit the hardwood floor. The heat of the tears streaming down her cheeks surprised her. The man with whom she'd shared the last ten years of her life didn't even bother to close the door as he walked out of her life.

Chapter **3**

(Four months later)

Geeter popped the top on a bottle of hard cider. The sweet vapors that rose from it tickled his nose. With a kind word to the patron, he placed the cold brown bottle on a napkin. The cool wetness of the bar towel felt good in his hands. Though mid-April, the warmth of the day had brought out little beads of sweat on his forehead. It was still a week or two before his boss would turn on the A/C.

A loud whistle brought his eyes to his boss, who stood halfway down the stairs. Geeter's smile didn't stay there long. Something wasn't right. John's face was somber as he motioned for Geeter to join him in the upstairs office. *I do something wrong?* Shrugging, he didn't worry about it until John closed the door, pointing to a seat.

There was a slight quiver in his boss's voice. "Gideon..." *That's my real name.* He never called Geeter by his first name, except when he screwed up. Geeter's body tensed as he prepared to get chewed out.

John gripped the back of his chair momentarily before continuing. "Gideon, I just got off the phone with your sister. I have some, uh, some very bad news for you. Your parents..." He stopped and cleared his throat.

"...Your parents were killed in a car accident this morning."

What? Mom, Daddy gone? His body turned cold, despite the warmth of the room. Geeter's eyes blurred. He tried to breathe through his nose, but his nostrils were suddenly wet.

Geeter felt John place an arm around his shoulder. "Get your things. I'll drive you to your sister's place."

He hesitated. "No. Sarah lives in Chattanooga, three hours away. Too far. I'll... I'll drive it myself."

"I don't mind. You shouldn't be alone at a time like this."

"S'okay. I wanna be alone." *Please let me be for a few minutes.*

"Would you like me to step out and give you some privacy?"

Geeter couldn't quite form the words, so he nodded. He held it together until the door closed.

By now, his cheeks were wet. Guilt filled his soul. His parents had begged him to come home last weekend because he hadn't been home since Christmas. *Instead, I spent the weekend here to go on a date, another failed date.* A vision of his mom and daddy filled his mind. His heart pounded painfully in his chest at the thought he'd never see them again. The creeping feeling of fear started up his spine and down his arms. Loud, angry voices screamed in his head. Same ones that had erupted after losing his entire team in Iraq. It was happening again. He needed help. He needed to hear the voice of the man who had talked him off the ledge when he'd almost lost his mind, when he'd almost ended it all.

His hands were shaking so bad, he dialed the number wrong four times before getting it right. The phone had barely rung when a pleasant woman's voice greeted him, "Geeter! Long time, no talk. How's my favorite bartender?" Katie's voice was warm, happy and full of joy, just like it had been on the day he'd met her, a direct contrast to what he was feeling.

He was quiet for a moment as he struggled to fight back the sob that was waiting to escape. Still, when he spoke, his voice betrayed the effort. "Katie, is... is L.T., is L.T. there?"

She hesitated. "Of course. Everything okay?"

"No. No, Mom and Daddy, Mom and Daddy are, are... they're dead."

"Oh my God. I'll get him right now. Hold on."

If anyone would understand his loss, it would be Jeremy. He'd lost his parents, too. And men under his command. He would help. Jeremy knew how to slay the demons.

Jeremy's calm, strong voice came on the cell. "Katie told me what happened. How can I help? Say the word and we'll be on our way to you."

***

Geeter stepped out of his truck at his sister Sarah's house, kicking aside gravel as he walked. She gripped the porch rail. Even in the dim evening light, her eyes were puffed, cheeks red. The stairs creaked when he climbed onto the porch. Sarah's face saddened as she reached for him. He held her tightly for a long time in the deepening darkness. They didn't say a word, didn't have to. Their hug was all the comfort they had.

The next few days were a blur. Geeter put up a good front for his sister, but he was numb inside during the funeral and the wake. His good friends, Kaitlin and Jeremy Roberts, were there, helping with any and everything that they could. Now they stood on the porch, preparing to say goodbye.

Kaitlin kissed his cheek then whispered, "You're never alone. Remember we love you. Call us anytime, day or night if you need us, okay?"

He extended his hand to Jeremy, his former lieutenant from his army days.

Jeremy grasped Geeter's hand and pulled him into a firm embrace. Jeremy thumped his fist against Geeter's back. "I'm here, my friend. Anytime you need me. If it gets too hard, call and I'll come down."

Sarah held Geeter's hand as they watched the Roberts drive off. Her husband, Burt, came onto the porch with a pitcher of tea.

The slamming of the screen door echoed in Geeter's mind as if it were a hand grenade. Sarah took his arm, leading him to the glider. The scent of Burt's coon hounds wafted up from the old musty cushion.

Sarah held her brother's hand. "On Friday, we'll meet with the lawyer to go over the will. Mom and Daddy left the farm to both of us, so we have a decision to make. Burt and I aren't farm people. If you want it, we'll be partners and help out, but if not, we need to think about selling it."

Do I want the farm? The scent of freshly pulled sweet corn filled his nose. Memories of picking strawberries with his daddy in the hot spring sun were as real as if he had just come in from the field. The taste of berries filled his mouth. His fingers suddenly felt sticky. When he opened his eyes, he expected his fingers to be red from the fruit. His mother's voice softly echoed in his mind, calling him to the table for fresh strawberry cornbread. His heart broke all over again as he realized he would never hear her voice, ever.

He stood and walked to the railing. He caught a glimpse of the evening's first star. "We can't sell our home, Sarah. That's all that's left of Mom and Daddy! How could we..." His voice wavered.

He walked to the corner of the porch as the last colors of the day faded away, so his sister couldn't see his face. *Why didn't I come home when they asked me to?*

The emptiness of his loss hurt, as if someone had ripped his heart out of his chest. "I was such a horrible son, such a failure. So involved in my own life that I ignored them. They must have hated me."

Sarah wrapped her arms around him. Her voice was choppy with emotion. "You're wrong, brother. They's so proud of you. Daddy was always bragging you up as a war hero. And Mom? She loved you the best. Couldn't never quit talking 'bout you. They loved you very much." Her words of comfort brought a fresh set of tears. It hurt like someone had cut his heart from his chest with a dull knife.

A hoot owl was calling in the distance when they finished talking. Geeter glanced at his watch—2:15 A.M. But it was all agreed upon. Geeter would move home and take care of the family farm. It was a gigantic truck patch, 273 acres of vegetables and farm crops, most already planted. The strawberries were close to being ripe.

Going home. Would it really ever be a home again? Only time would tell.

Chapter 4

K elly checked her makeup one final time before she turned to her sister Kaitlin. It felt odd to wear makeup again. "Well, how do I look?"

Kaitlin smiled. "As always, you look absolutely stunning! Like Daddy says, prettiest girl in the family. You'll knock 'em dead. Ready for your interview?"

Kelly shivered. A rogue chill slithered up her spine. "Guess I'm about as ready as I'll ever be." She hugged her sister. "Wish me luck." She drew back and the love in her sister's eyes caused a lump to rise in Kelly's throat. She grasped Kaitlin's hand.

"Good luck, Kel, but you won't need it. You got this."

Kelly needed to say it. "Before I go, I want to thank you and Jeremy for everything you've done. Moving me in here, helping to take care of the kids and me. After what Ballister..." Her voice started to crackle.

Kaitlin lightly shook her shoulders. "Stop it! Just stop it! We said today was an idiot-free day so quit thinking about him, okay?"

"I know, I know, but even though he doesn't love me, I still love him."

"I understand how tough it must be on you. Can't begin to fathom what you're going through. Love you."

Warmth flowed through Kaitlin's hands. "And you don't know how thankful I am for that. Having you as my sister is the greatest blessing in my life. You and Jeremy and Mom and Dad, you've all been so good to us. That's what allows me the strength to get up each morning. Don't think I'd have made it this far without you."

Kaitlin smiled. "That's what family's for. We love you! Always have, always will."

Kelly kissed her sister's cheek before departing for the hospital.

***

Kelly's interview was for a geriatric nursing position on the sixth floor of Chicago General Hospital. She'd been the Clinical Nurse Manager for the Emergency Department in her last job. This position should be a piece of cake. She hoped it wouldn't be boring.

It had been seven years since she last interviewed. Arriving early at the HR Department, she was ushered into a conference room where the interview team waited. The tingling of anxiety vanished as they peppered her with questions and scenarios. Her mind shifted back into nursing gear. Before she knew it, the familiar scents of disinfectant and charts lifted her spirits and the geriatric floor's clinical manager gave her a tour of the sixth floor. The interview had gone better than she ever dreamed possible.

"So, Ms. Jenkins, what do you think?"

"Please call me Kelly. Seems to be a good organization and great teamwork on the unit."

"I agree. So... Want to be part of our team?"

Kelly turned to stare at her. "Are you offering me the position?"

The manager smiled. "Sure am, Kelly. You can start next Monday, evening shift. Want to join the team?"

Pride filled her heart as she extended her hand. "Yes. Thank you."

***

Kelly's hands were shaking when she walked off the elevator. The clinical manager was waiting at the unit clerk's desk. "Hi, Kelly. I'd like to introduce you to Alise. You'll be shadowing her for the first shift or two."

Kelly smiled at the younger girl. As Alise scanned Kelly from head to toe, it became apparent she didn't like what she saw. *Ah, the cattiness of the younger generation. Didn't miss that at all.* Disappointment filled Kelly's mind. The RN was at least ten years younger and, as Kelly discovered as the shift progressed, woefully inexperienced.

The lack of experience became painfully evident five hours into the shift. Kelly was about to take vitals on a patient when Alise's phone alarmed. "Code blue, room 6256. Code blue, room 6256." While Alise hesitated, Kelly reacted quickly, running to the room. The younger nurse followed her.

Kelly scanned the monitors. The patient was flatlined. She moved into position to begin CPR, but Alise pushed her aside. "You need to follow protocol." Kelly's blood started to boil as she realized Alise was checking for vital signs. *Look at the monitor! His heart stopped, idiot.* Alise grabbed his chart and started reading aloud, "Patient is eighty-five years old. Type II diabetic with allergies to—"

Kelly shoved her out of the way. After clearing his airway, she handed Alise an Ambu bag while starting chest compressions. Kelly screamed, "Code Blue, Code Blue! Can we get some help in here?"

She was in her third minute of CPR when help finally arrived. The floor charge nurse and two other nurses suddenly appeared with the crash cart. A tall man in a white coat followed them in, but didn't interrupt. Kelly was glad when the charge nurse ordered them to stop. Her arms and back ached from the exertion.

The charge nurse pointed to the monitor. "He's back!" The patient's heart was again beating and, while labored, he was breathing on his own. The charge nurse pumped her fists in the air. "Great job, nurses!"

Kelly and Alise walked out. The young RN's breathing was rapid, and she looked very pale. "I think I need a couple of minutes," she told Kelly without making eye contact.

Kelly felt sorry for her. "Take all the time you need, sister. I got the med pass." Kelly returned to her med cart, where the reassuring coolness and scent of hand sanitizer soothed her. *I missed this. What God intended me to do.* She smiled as she prepared meds for the next patient.

After taking the patient's pulse and administering Digoxin to a heart patient, she returned to the hallway. Leaning against her med cart was the tall man in the white coat. He smiled as he extended his hand.

His eyes twinkled. She had never seen a man with teeth so white. For a second, she wondered if they would sparkle like the ones on the old toothpaste commercials. Kelly took his hand. *So soft and warm, like a newborn puppy.* Her mouth was suddenly dry.

The man's deep voice derailed her train of thoughts. "Saw the whole thing in there. You were the one who saved his life. Great job, Nurse...?"

"Jenkins, Kelly Jenkins."

"Good work, Nurse Jenkins. That was impressive. I'm Dr. Andrews, Todd Andrews."

"Thank you, doctor."

His eyes seemed to bore into her soul, like he was exploring her from the inside out. She felt the urge to pull her sweater across her chest to protect her modesty.

"New here? Don't think I've met you before."

He throws a pickup line at me? Kelly laughed and his eyes opened widely, as if he wanted to drink in all of her aura. "Actually, Dr. Andrews, it's my first night."

His whistled softly before exclaiming, "Wow! First night and already saving lives! Guess Chicago General got pretty lucky when they hired you."

Kelly blushed. "Thank you."

Dr. Andrews looked at his watch. "Say, Nurse Jenkins, like to grab a cup of coffee?"

He has cute eyes, but no. Something rose inside Kelly, something warm. "I can't. I still have meds to push and then mountains of charting to do. You know how it goes."

He looked a little sad, but nodded. "Okay, Nurse Jenkins, some other time." He started to go, but turned to face her. "May I call you Kelly? Well, not in front of patients, but when it's only you and me?"

She smiled as she nodded yes.

"And please, call me Todd, when there aren't others around. 'Night!" With a smile and a wink, he walked off.

Chapter 5

K elly quickly fell into the routine of her job, rotating days, nights, evenings, and weekends.

Dr. Andrews showed up at least once during every one of her shifts, even when she was pulling nights. He became the bright spot in her days. His smile captivated her. His cologne reminded her of warm ocean breezes. But his eyes...

Their conversations always seemed to begin when he walked past her and then turned. "Say, aren't you that lifesaving nurse, what was the name, uh, Nurse Wonder Woman?"

Kelly's heart fluttered. "Why, no, sir. Name's Jenkins. And you are? Never was good at names."

He flashed that dazzling smile. "You don't remember? I know we've met. I would hope I made a good impression."

She would put her hand to her mouth as if she were trying to remember. "You do look slightly familiar. Was the name John Doe?"

His eyes would crinkle. "Dr. John Doe, but you can call me anything you like, as long as you have that cup of coffee with me."

She would purse her lips, but they always betrayed her by breaking into a smile. "I'll think about it."

Andrews would wag his finger. "I'm persistent, so you better say yes. You will one day, I guarantee you that."

After this ritual, they would engage in small talk. Kelly loved it. She was beginning to know him. Almost like putting together a jigsaw puzzle, piece by piece. And she liked what she saw. She wanted to know everything about him, but her mind forced her to take it slow. The wound Ballister had left on her heart was still too fresh.

***

Kelly didn't think anything of Todd showing up all the time until she overheard a conversation at the nursing station between one of the nurses and the unit clerk. They obviously didn't know she was checking inventory in the small storage locker behind the nurse's station.

"Did you see Doctor Hotbuns showed up again today?"

"Of course he did. And you know why, don't you? Miss Perfect is working."

"You mean Jenkins? I hate her. Such a bitch, always looking down her nose at us. Thinks she's so much better than everyone else. Stuck up know-it-all. What in the world does he see in her?"

"You mean beyond her long blonde hair, pretty face, and hour-glass figure? He must want her for her mind!" They shared an evil laugh. "Think she knows he's the medical director for the sixth floor?"

"Of course she does. She's probably sleeping with him, and before you know it, she'll be in charge of the floor."

"Well, when you don't have talent or skills, putting out is always a good option."

Kelly had enough. Her blood was steaming as she walked up behind them. "Hi, girls! Who you talking about?" The look on their faces was priceless. "Oh, were the two of you talking about me?" She feigned being shocked. Silence ensued as they both suddenly became engrossed in paperwork. Kelly's face burned while her anger boiled over.

She stomped to the front of the unit desk and slammed her hands down to get their attention. "So, you girls have nothing better to do than gossip about me, eh? No talent? Is that what you really believe? And you think I have to sleep my way to the top?"

Kelly menacingly walked around the desk. The two girls started to back away. "Let me tell you bitches something. You can't lead when you're on your back. You lead by example. I was the Clinical Nursing Manager for the entire Emergency Department at my last hospital. I earned everything I achieved in life. If you two think I had to sleep my way anywhere, you can kiss my ass." She kicked over the waste can. "Find something meaningful to do now, or I'll find something for you."

Kelly stormed off to her med cart. After unlocking it, she slammed the keys on its top. *Catty little worthless bitches.*

Less than five minutes later, Dr. Andrews appeared at her side. He walked past before turning to her. "Say, aren't you that lifesaving nurse, what was the name, uh, nurse Wonder Woman?"

From the corner of her eye, Kelly noted her accusers huddled together at the nurse's station, watching. No doubt they were talking about her. She waved at them, noting they suddenly got busy. Turning to Dr. Andrews, she said, "I'm ready for that coffee. Offer still there?"

Andrews' eyes went wide. "Of course."

Kelly smiled. "Shift's over in an hour. Let me see if I can get a sitter."

Chapter 6

A quick call to Kaitlin sealed the babysitter deal. Kelly was grateful that her parents, sister, and brother-in-law were always willing to watch the kids. She forced back guilt every night she worked second shift because she missed bath and story time. On those nights, Kaitlin seemed to be taking the role of 'Mommy' to her kids. And her little one, David, had started calling Jeremy, 'Daddy.'

She reached the café. The scent of coffee gave her courage. A patron walked in, sporting a blond goatee. Reminded her of Ballister and how her ex-husband had just walked away from all of them for that slutty actress. She'd been on TV the other day, and there he was, holding her arm. The wound was starting to heal as the scab toughened. Those two girls at work weren't the only ones who could...

At that moment, Todd Andrews drifted into the café, scanning the seats. When his eyes found hers, his face lit up with a million-dollar smile that raised her core temperature.

He stopped in front of her. "Hey, Kelly! Now that we're out of the hospital, I can finally tell you that I think you look beautiful tonight."

Kelly's cheeks warmed. "Thank you."

He winked. "Time for that infamous cup of coffee. Finally! My treat tonight."

After they ordered, they sat and talked, so easily, so naturally. One thing raised a small flag in Kelly's mind though. Todd asked her lots of questions, but closely guarded any information about himself. He had a great tableside manner, and before long, she found herself telling her entire story.

"I met Kelly Ballister at college."

"Wait. You married a man named Kelly?" He smiled. "Let me guess. You named your firstborn Kelly, too."

Smart aleck. "Matter of fact, our oldest son is named Kelly Junior, but I call him K.J."

His smile left. "Sorry. Trying to be funny."

She shot him a wink. "You're funny all right, funny looking."

He laughed. "He's stupid, you know."

"Come again?"

"For leaving you. He'll regret it."

The comment made her eyes scratchy. "Didn't seem to regret it at all."

Todd swirled his cup before taking another sip. "He'll beg you to take him back someday. Do me a favor."

Favor? "Like what?"

"Don't take him back." His gaze was piercing, making her feel as if she were naked. Once again, she pulled her sweater closed so it covered her chest. His eyes didn't leave hers.

"May I make a toast?" He held up his latte. "To great beginnings and hopefully a long and wonderful friendship."

She raised her cup, "So what about you? You haven't said much. You a secret agent?"

"No. Just not very interesting. Undergrad work at Ohio State, med school at Purdue, internship at Chicago General, and voila, here I am."

"You have a practice outside the hospital?"

"Yep, Chicago Center for Geriatrics."

She twirled her mocha around. The kaleidoscope of butterflies in her stomach grew. His brown eyes twinkled with delight. "Why'd you pick geriatrics?"

"My granddad. Developed dementia at an early age. It tore up my grandma, actually it affected my entire family. I wanted to use my skills to make a difference in the lives of people who suffered from that horrible disease."

Wow. Bet you rescue baby seals on your day off, too. She appreciated his devotion. Suddenly, Kelly changed the subject. "Todd, I have a pointed question to ask you. Why is it that you seem to be at the hospital every time I'm working? I heard you're the medical director for the sixth floor. Is that why, or is there some other reason?"

He blushed slightly, studying his drink before answering. His eyes didn't quite meet hers. "My duties do require me to be on the floor frequently, but that's not really why I show up. There is a personal reason, and I believe you know what the reason is, Ms. Jenkins."

Her heart rate increased. "Well, Dr. John Doe, exactly what is that personal reason?"

His blush deepened. "I want to be totally transparent." He raised his eyes to engage hers. "It's because I want to see you. I have access to the nursing schedule, so I make sure I get into the hospital every time you work."

She had suspected, even hoped that was why, but hearing him put it into words warmed her heart. It was Kelly's turn to blush.

He glanced at his watch. "I'm sorry, Kelly, but I have an appointment. May I see you again?"

"Another cup of coffee?"

"Actually I was thinking about dinner. I know this is your weekend off, and I was wondering if you would go out with me Saturday afternoon."

Kelly bit her lip. She liked him and really hoped it might turn into more, but now that the offer was there, she was scared.

When she didn't answer, he studied the tiled floor. "I see you might have some things you need to work through." He took out a slip of paper and wrote down his cell number. "Please think about it and text me, okay?" He extended his hand, finishing with, "I hope you say yes. I really want to see you again. 'Night."

After he left, she studied her coffee. Her mocha had been cocoa colored before, but was much darker now. *Funny how things can change right before your eyes.* Was her life changing before her eyes? She didn't know.

Chapter 7

G eeter straightened up, hands rubbing his aching back after placing the last box in the truck bed. The sun glinting off the sheet metal on the shed almost blinded him. He was a farmer now, a simple farmer. Long days, up early, no rest even when weary. *One thing about it, always something to do.* He covered the bed of the pickup, then checked his watch. He needed to deliver this load of peas to the local farmer's market before they opened. The twenty-minute trip would be a good time to give Jeremy a call.

Jeremy and his pretty wife Katie had been a godsend. Trying to work through his parents' untimely deaths had been rough. The pair were there, always listening, always positive, always encouraging. Jeremy had it made, really had it together. He was the luckiest man alive to be married to that little girl with the face of an angel and a heart of gold.

The scent of fresh cut hay soothed Geeter's mind as he relaxed his grip on the wheel. He waited for an answer on the other end of the line. The call opened with the sound of children laughing and singing. Jeremy's voice came on, "Hey, bubba. What's shaking?'"

"Mornin', L.T. What's goin' on in Chicago?"

"Not much. Katie and I are taking my sister-in-law's kids out to breakfast."

The sweet voice of Kaitlin came across the air, "Hey, Geeter. How's my favorite farmer?"

Geeter smiled. Katie, always so bubbly. *Why can't I find a girl like her?* "I's doin' fine. It's awful purty down here. Y'all should come visit a spell."

Kaitlin laughed at his exaggerated accent. "Maybe this summer. Melinda! Stop hitting your sister. K.J.! Quit instigating. I saw that! Sorry, Geeter. Kids, you know?"

Something formed at the back of his throat. *Always wanted a passel of kids.* That would never happen. He was horrible with women. Hadn't been on a second date since college. Before the bastards slammed those planes into the Towers. Before he...

"Now listen to your Aunt Katie or I'll turn this truck around and we'll sit at the table and wait for the Cubs to win the World Series." The noise on the line dropped. "Didn't think so. That's better. So how was your week?"

"Good. Taking the first picking of peas to town. Oh, L.T., guess what!"

"What?"

"Never believe what I found in the old chicken house."

"I don't know. Uh, a goose that lays golden eggs?"

"Nope. I found Rita."

Jeremy's voice revealed disbelief. "Rita? I thought she was gone for good."

"Nope. She's there."

"How'd you find her?"

"Looking for some rock guards for the sickle mower. Daddy had lots of stuff crammed there. Was going through boxes when I realized there was somethin' firm under the tarp. Looked underneath, and there she was."

Kaitlin's voice was next. "Rita? Who's Rita? I don't understand."

Jeremy was laughing. "Rita is Geeter's first love."

The roar of an Allis Chalmers tractor passing on the other side of the road drowned out the conversation for a few seconds.

"No, honey. His first car, not his first girlfriend."

Geeter smiled ear to ear, remembering when he'd first found her. "Not just any car, Katie. She's a '71 Dodge Challenger R/T with a hemi engine. Almost forgot about her. She was as filthy as a pig, but ran as good as when Daddy and I fixed her up. Bought her when I was sixteen."

Kaitlin laughed. "You're getting this excited over some old car?"

"Honey, you just don't understand what Rita means to Geeter. It would be the same to you as... as... say, your first prom dress."

Kaitlin responded as if Jeremy had offended her. "What? Because I'm a woman, I can't possibly fathom the memories a first car can bring out in a man? And as far as a prom dress, you know I never went to prom. Perhaps you need to practice your active listening skills a little more."

"Sorry. What'd you say?"

Geeter's spirit rose listening to these two people who were madly in love. "Katie, Rita's special because she was ten minutes away from enterin' junkyard heaven when me and Daddy bought her. It's not so much the car as it was the times we shared gettin' her fixed. Know what I mean?"

They talked for another ten minutes before he arrived at the farmer's market. Unloading the cases of peas quickly, he headed back home. Busy or not, he decided to make time to take Rita out.

He slid into the bucket seat, the scent of cherry air freshener taking him back in time. The car had once represented freedom from the life of a farmer. Now, she represented ties to the past. He had painstakingly gone over every inch of Rita, making her look and sound like she had when he'd tarped her before enlisting.

The 426 hemi engine roared as he pointed Rita toward Lookout Mountain. The apple-blossom-tinged air filled him with hope. His life was finally heading in the right direction. His heart felt it. He stopped Rita at a 'Y' in the road at the bottom of the mountain. Which way should he go? Didn't seem to matter, both ways were looking up. He just had to choose the direction that was right for him.

Chapter 8

K elly arrived home just in time for bedtime stories, prayers and goodnight kisses. The bedroom doors were barely closed when Kaitlin grabbed her hand, pulling her out to the front porch swing. "Okay, sis, spill the beans!"

Kelly's cheeks warmed. "I don't know what you mean."

"Aw, come on! Tell me all about your date."

The scent of mulch from the recently worked flowerbeds tickled her nose. "Not too much to tell, really."

"Right. Nice try. I know you better than anyone. You've got a glow about you. Come on, tell me, tell me, tell me! You know I'd tell you."

"Really? Then explain that glow you and Jeremy had this morning."

"Okay. That's fair. This morning before we came downstairs, Jeremy and I..."

Kelly threw up her hands. "Stop. You win." Kaitlin knew how to push her buttons. Kelly opened up, telling Kaitlin about the whole day, including the nasty conversation she'd overheard at the nurse's station, followed by a recap of everything Todd said. She mentioned not only how hot he looked, but how he made her melt inside.

"See, that wasn't so bad, was it?"

Breathlessness surfaced at the back of her throat as her hands sweated. "Katie, there's more."

Kaitlin's eyebrows raised. "Like?"

Kelly bit her lip. "He asked me out for next Saturday."

"What did you say?"

Tension built in her arms and hands. "I didn't say anything. I don't have a sitter."

"You do now."

"Or anything to wear."

"Ransack my closet. We're the same size. If that doesn't work, we'll go shopping."

"Or..."

"We'll take care of that, too."

The scent of Kaitlin's perfume floated gently in the air. "You don't even know what I was going to say."

Kaitlin chuckled. "I'm not going to let you find an excuse to avoid happiness."

"You're pushy."

"You taught me."

"Have an answer for everything, don't you?"

"Yep. Taught me that, too."

***

Kelly waited on a bench outside a nice restaurant close to the mall. The scent of freshly cut grass reminded her of cool watermelon on a hot day. Todd pulled up in a silver BMW, a small bouquet of flowers in his hand.

His eyes sparkled as he stood before her. "You look beautiful, Kelly. Why is it every time I see you, you look prettier than the time before?"

Her cheeks warmed. "And you look quite charming as well, Dr. Doe."

He rolled his eyes. "Compliments will get you anything you desire, Nurse Wonder Woman." Their conversation was nonstop during the meal, even though it was all about Kelly and work. Following dessert, they crossed the street to take a walk in the park.

The unexpected warmth of the day made her skin glisten as they strolled. Somewhere near the middle of the walk, Todd's hand brushed hers. Without a word, he laced his fingers through hers. Every nerve in her body tingled. *I can feel your heartbeat, quick and strong.* His hands were so much larger than Ballister's. Larger, but so soft and comforting.

At the end of the walk, he turned to her. Sadness seemed to flow out of him. "I'm going to visit family this week. I'll miss you."

Kelly's shoulder muscles tensed. "Miss you, too. How long?"

"Flying back Saturday morning. May I take you to dinner Saturday night?"

She suddenly had to restrain her neck muscles because they wanted to lean in to kiss him. She nodded involuntarily. "I'd love that."

Todd walked her to her car, kissing her fingertips before closing the driver's door.

***

Her work week was long and lonely without Todd stopping by to say hello. Arriving for the evening shift on Wednesday, she found a large bouquet of flowers waiting for her. The scent of red roses was fresh and crisp and enticing. Her coworkers kept asking who the flowers were from, but she told them she didn't know. "Wouldn't be surprised if they're from my children." She slipped the card into her pocket before any prying eyes could peek.

***

Her legs and feet ached as she stumbled up the stairs to her room. It had been a long, hard shift and she was looking forward to reading the card in her pocket. She suspected, well, hoped, the flowers were from Todd. Her entire body tingled as she read the greeting. "Nurse Wonder Woman, I miss seeing your beautiful smile and pretty face. But even more, I miss the sound of your voice. I've grown so accustomed to seeing you, I think I'm having withdrawal. What do you suggest? (wink, wink, nudge, nudge) Looking forward to Saturday when I can be with you. I miss you! Doctor John Doe."

Pain brewed in the pit of her stomach. She missed him so much. The burning desire in her heart was also becoming painfully obvious. *Love? Is this real or just...* She wasn't sure. It had been so long since she'd dated. She had always hated dating and the games that went with it. Her mind informed her that sleep was not going to come until she talked about it. *Katie's probably sleeping.* The conversation between her heart and mind left her as a spectator. *She said she'd be there anytime and for any reason.* But it's after midnight. *Who cares? Wake her up!*

Walking down the hallway to the room Kaitlin and Jeremy shared, she stopped and listened at the door. No noise. *Good.* Kelly opened the door slowly, whispering, "Katie?" A sudden movement of two people jumping into the bed caught her attention. She turned away when she realized Kaitlin and Jeremy had been awake... and naked. She had interrupted their lovemaking.

Jeremy whispered sharply, "What's going on? Kids okay?"

She was glad the lights were off. If the heat on her cheeks was any indication, she'd discovered a new shade of blush. *Can't believe I walked in on them while they were...* "They're fine. Sorry to interrupt. Hoping I could borrow your wife, but I see now isn't a good time. I apologize for not knocking first." She turned to go.

Kaitlin giggled as she grabbed her teddy from the floor. She slipped it on and donned a robe. "It's okay." Kaitlin kissed Jeremy. "Be back soon. Rest up. We'll pick up where we left off. That's a promise."

Out in the hallway, Kaitlin turned to her sister. "What's wrong, Kel?"

"I'm sorry, but I need someone to talk to, and this isn't Mom-appropriate. Sure you don't mind? I didn't mean to interrupt."

Kaitlin smiled, "It's okay. I needed a break anyway. Jeremy is wearing me out trying to get me pregnant. Let's go downstairs and talk."

The lingering smell of last night's lasagna filled the kitchen. The sisters nuked the leftovers, pulling two diet Pepsis out of the fridge.

Kaitlin watched her as they ate in silence. "What's going on?"

"Sorry to bother you. I'm rusty when it comes to this whole dating thing. Todd sent me flowers at work... and listen to his note." Kelly read the card. "I don't know what to do. I still love Ballister, but I'm attracted, very attracted to Todd. I'm starting to feel like there could be something special happening between us, but I don't know."

"Don't know what?"

Kelly had trouble swallowing the soda. *Moment of truth.* "If I'm falling in love or not."

Kaitlin brushed her sister's hair from her eyes. "Yes, you do. I think feelings for your ex-idiot are clouding your mind. Listen to me! Ballister left you, Kelly." Kaitlin paused for effect.

"I'm painfully aware of that."

"I'm not trying to be mean, but you did everything you could have to save your marriage. He didn't care.

News flash, sis. Life goes on. Don't you dare feel guilty for wanting to find happiness. If seeing where it goes with Todd brings you happiness, you should find out."

Kelly started to protest, "But..."

Kaitlin grabbed her wrists. "Stop it. I know you better than anyone ever did. You're full of love and kindness inside. Such a very wonderful person. You deserve the best."

"Katie..."

Kaitlin continued. "God has a grand master plan. Sometimes, to find true happiness, we have to go through miserable things. I know I did. You know what hell I went through. That made me throw a shield up around my heart, to prevent any man from getting inside it."

Her sister was right. Not long ago, the roles were reversed. Kelly was the one giving Kaitlin advice. "I remember."

"Then Jeremy saved me during the worst moment of my life. That was God's plan for me. If it hadn't happened just like it did, my heart would still be shielded. I wouldn't have discovered Jeremy was the one God intended for me."

"But you didn't know that."

"No, I didn't. But God did."

"But how can I tell if it's love or not?"

Kaitlin held her, shushing her fears. "There's no guarantee. You have to experience life to live it. My advice? Live, love, and have faith. You deserve happiness. It's coming. Do you hear me?"

Katie should be a motivational speaker. Warmth flowed through Kelly's body. She smiled. "Yes, I do."

Chapter 9

The scent of sizzling beef filled the restaurant. Kelly was oblivious to it. She was already seated at the table when Todd walked in. He scanned the dining area, but when he saw her, his face lit up. Kelly's breath caught. *God, I missed him.* She stood, waiting for his greeting. Without saying a word, he slipped his arms around her. His touch sent tingles of excitement across her back. They hugged long and hard. Breaking away, she gazed into the brown eyes she had missed all week.

"Hey, Nurse Wonder Woman."

"Hello, Doctor Doe."

Todd slowly lowered his lips toward her, stopping to rub the tip of his nose against hers.

A battle raged inside her. *Too soon*, screamed her mind. *Don't let this opportunity pass,* replied her heart. As his lips continued the descent toward hers, she met him there. Her heart had won.

His lips tasted like mint, and for a second, the vision of a bright moon over a beautiful sea swallowed her. His lips were so soft. Every muscle in her body relaxed as he held her in his arms. *This is perfect.* After he pulled away slowly, her lips begged for more. When she opened her eyes to his vibrant smile, she could swear his teeth sparkled. He held her chair for her.

Sitting across the table, he reached for her hands and held them tightly. "I missed you so much. Tell me about your week."

"Honestly, it was a very lonely week. I kept looking up, wishing you would appear. And the day you sent me the flowers? That was the hardest day of all. You don't know what they meant to me."

He smiled. The corners of his eyes curved as if mimicking his lips. "Glad you liked them. Were they pretty?"

Now that he was finally here, she was having trouble concentrating. The sweetness of the kiss still lingered on her lips. She wanted more. "The bouquet was gorgeous."

He gently touched his lips to her fingertips. Fiery feelings of pleasure ran up her arm, straight to her heart.

"No flower could ever match your beauty. Your skin is flawless. Your face beyond compare. Your voice, like an angel chorus. If I could dream up the perfect woman, it would be you."

Before Kelly could answer, the waiter arrived. The conversation was soft and easy as they waited for their food. The butterflies in her stomach affected her appetite. She was more interested in Todd than the food.

"Not hungry tonight, huh?"

No, I'm more interested in you. "For whatever reason, no."

"Hopefully the company didn't affect your appetite, did it?"

Kelly laughed. "Of course not." *Okay, I just lied.*

"Would you like to see a movie? I hear there's a good romantic comedy that just came out. Want to see it?"

I would watch paint dry, just to be with you. "Um hum."

The floor was sticky from spilled soda. Fugitive popcorn kernels congregated in the seam of the seat. Kelly couldn't have cared less. Todd had his arm around her, and at a funny moment in the movie, she turned to say something. As she did, Todd leaned in and kissed her softly. She responded by placing her arms around his neck to return the kiss. He worked his lips across her neck, nibbling on her earlobe. The excitement building in her body was clouding her sense of judgment. Her heart was suggesting things she hadn't done in months.

Her breath was coming in joyous bursts. "Please stop."

"Why?"

Her head was spinning, whether from his aftershave or his kisses, she didn't know. "Because..."

Todd gently held her face in his hands, his eyes burning away her courage to say no by the second. "Because you don't like it... or because you do?"

She couldn't resist. She kissed him hard and long. When her lungs felt as if they would explode, she pulled away and whispered in his ear, "Because if you keep this up, I won't be able to resist."

His face turned serious. "Let's go back to my place. I'll kiss away the last shreds of your resistance."

No, no. Too soon. "I can't."

"Why not? You know my touch turns you on, and I can guarantee, I can't recall ever being this excited."

The look in Todd's eyes changed. Love had changed to lust. Kelly stiffened. She needed to leave. "Sorry, but I can't." She grabbed her purse, preparing to go.

The viselike grip of his hand pinched her skin. "Please don't tell me you're going to leave me when I'm this turned on. I'm ready to explode. If you care about me at all, don't go."

"I'm sorry." Kelly kissed him quickly before running out of the theater. Ten more seconds of his lips on her neck, and she would have said yes to anything, and everything.

Chapter 10

D r. Andrews failed to show up during Kelly's shift for the next several weeks. Her mind said, *He only wanted to use me.* But her heart disagreed. The pain of withdrawal was as bad as when she had kicked the smoking habit years ago. Her chest ached because she missed Todd.

All four of her children came down with a nasty stomach virus in late August. Kelly took a few days off to be with them. Lacking the vacation time that came with seniority, she had to pull a few extra shifts to get in her hours.

Her eyelids were rebelling from having to stay open so long. Why she'd ever agreed to pull a double shift escaped her reasoning. When the digital clock changed from 2:59 to 3:00, she hoisted her bag on her shoulder.

The charge nurse called to her, "Thanks for helping out. Want me to call security to have them escort you to your car? Parking garage is kind of lonely this time of night."

Kelly shook her head. "I'll be fine." Leaning against the corner of the elevator car, it was hard to fight off sleep. The acrid scent of urine permeated the air. *Can't wait to change and shower.*

The dinging of the elevator indicated she'd reached the parking level. The automated monorail from the hospital to the parking garage was deserted. Perched in a corner seat in the first car, she could see the entire train. The recorded voice warning to stand clear of the doors hurt her ears because no other bodies were there to absorb the soundwaves.

Kelly had an itchy spot on her right cheek. *Need to look at that when I get home.* She dug her keys out of her purse, as well as the pepper spray she carried for late, lonely nights. She placed the spray canister in the pocket of her scrub top.

The trip was short, as always. Checking her surroundings, she walked to the elevators. *Couple lights out. Need to report that to the safety committee.* The elevator was empty as she pressed the button for the fifth deck.

The elevator came to a smooth stop before the doors silently opened. Kelly scanned the floor before leaving the safety of the car. The sickly smell of rotting food mingled with the stale odor of discarded cigarettes in the smoke-free garage. In the distance, her trusty white Fusion was parked alone. The garage had been full when she arrived at 10:30 yesterday morning. She was about a third of the way to the Fusion when the soft sound of a closing car door caught her attention.

Every hair on her head seemed to stand up. She stopped to listen. Soft footfalls echoed behind her, then ceased. She started walking, quicker now. Her left hand gripped the key fob. Her right hand entered her scrub pocket, fingers fumbling to pop the plastic lid off. When it did, she gripped the canister in her fist, finger on the nozzle's trigger.

The footfalls were louder now. A tall man wearing a white lab coat lurked maybe ten feet behind her. She glanced over her shoulder. A scream rose in her throat. The Fusion was thirty feet away. She started to run, but a hand grabbed her left arm, spinning her around to face him. Kelly pressed the panic button on the Fusion's fob. The horn blared three times a second.

"Help! Help me!" Kelly screamed, her right hand now clearing her pocket. Her finger depressed the trigger as it moved. The man released her and covered his face with his arm as he hugged the floor. Kelly emptied the pepper spray at him and continued to scream for help.

"Stop, Kelly, stop! It's me, Todd."

Kelly stopped in mid-scream. "Is that really you?"

He rolled on the floor, tearing off his lab coat. He wiped furiously at his neck, where his exposed skin had taken the brunt of the acidic spray. "It's me. Please, no more. Damn, that burns."

The blaring horn of the Fusion was quite annoying. Kelly silenced it. "What the hell are you doing? Scared the daylights out of me!"

"I'll explain, but do you have any bottled water?"

Kelly produced a half empty bottle. Todd poured it on his affected skin, now quite red from the spray.

"I'm waiting for an explanation. You don't show up for weeks, then you stalk..."

"Wasn't stalking you. I was trying to get the courage up to apologize. When I found out you were working 'til 3:00 A.M., I wanted to make sure I was there so you got to your car safely."

Kelly's hands were shaking. From somewhere in the bowels of the garage, she could hear squealing wheels and a roaring engine. *Security.*

"Picked a rotten way to do it. Scared me almost out of my mind."

"Sorry, Kelly." He had to keep blinking his left eye, which was watering profusely. Some of the spray must have gotten in there. "More importantly, I'm sorry for the way I treated you on our date. Probably came across as someone who was only interested in one thing."

"Came across like a pervert. Then, you just vanished from my life."

"I was ashamed for treating someone as wonderful as you that way."

"Again, funny way of showing it."

"Can we start over? I miss you. I want to develop a special relationship with you."

"You mean a sexual relationship?"

"No. Kelly, I miss you. Seeing you, hearing you, knowing you. Give me another chance, please?"

The squealing tires were getting closer. The red and blue reflections of the emergency lights illuminated the deck. "What do you really want, Todd?"

He stood, left hand rubbing his eye. "Truth be told? I love you, Kelly. I'm hoping in time you'll love me, too."

"You don't show love by ignoring someone for two months."

"I know. Can we start over?"

Kelly started to search his eyes, but the roar of the engine and the flashing lights were joined by the sound of a newly engaged siren, drawing her attention. The answer that was on her lips stayed there. The security SUV swerved to a stop in front of them. Two guards poured out, rushing to get between Kelly and Todd.

"What's going on here?" Pointing at Todd, the guard screamed, "Get your hands up where I can see them."

Todd complied.

Kelly touched the guard's arm. "Misunderstanding, officer. Everything's fine."

The guard whipped toward her. "Everything's fine?"

Kelly's chest warmed, filling in the spot where despair had lived a few minutes ago. "Yes. Just a big misunderstanding."

"A big misunderstanding? You sure?"

Suddenly, the situation became comical. A full-bellied laugh started to work its way out. Kelly placed a hand over her mouth, but it spilled out. She nodded.

Todd stared at her in disbelief. "Everything's fine? You sure?"

Kelly nodded as she winked at him. "Yep. All one big, stupid misunderstanding. One that's in the past now."

Chapter 11

G eeter emptied the large water bottle in one long draw. He allowed some of the icy cold fluid to run out of the corner of his mouth, falling down to soak his filthy tee-shirt. Grabbing the loops on his jeans, he pulled them up before tightening the belt.

"Too big?"

Geeter smiled at Sarah. She worked so hard at the restaurant and here on the farm. But she always had time to watch out for her baby brother. "Yeah, need something smaller."

"You're wasting away to nothin'. How much you lost?"

"Near fifty pounds. All of it flab, though."

"I noticed. Maybe you should get Burt to help you. He could stand to lose a little weight."

Burt was walking out of the shed when the words left her lips. "Damn, woman. Ain't that the pot callin' the kettle black? You're twice as wide as when we got married."

"Know what that means, don't you?"

"Naw. What's that?"

"Twice as much to love, and don't you dare forget it." Sarah winked at Geeter as Burt headed back to the shed with the grease gun. Despite how they teased each other, Geeter knew they were deeply in love.

"Geeter?" Something in Sarah's tone caused him to stop and stare at her.

"What's wrong, sis?"

"Sit with me a spell, please?"

Something's wrong. Spiders were crawling up his spine. "'Kay. What's up?"

She smiled, spreading a ray of sunshine across his path. One of the good things that had come out of his parents' death was the rekindling of the close relationship they had as kids.

"Don't say it much, but I wanted to tell you I's proud of you." She tried to hide the quick movement of her hand wiping her eyes, but Geeter had noticed. He held her hand. "You remind me of Daddy sometimes. Workin' so hard. Keepin' everything together. It's like Mom and Daddy still live here." She wiped her eyes again.

His own eyes became scratchy. "Sarah. Wouldn't be possible without you."

She pushed his hand away. "One thing bothers me."

"What's that?"

"You work too hard. Never take time for yourself. We need to get you out of here once in a while."

Please, don't bring up women again. "I'm fine."

"You need a good girl in your life. There's this waitress at the restaurant who just got divorced..."

"Thought you said she was a good girl."

"She is. Just 'cause she's divorced don't mean..."

"Why'd she get divorced?"

"That good-for-nothing husband of hers cheated on her."

"Sarah. Might I remind you there's always two sides to every story?"

"And might I remind you man wasn't meant to live life alone? You need someone, a woman."

He shook his head. Tension was crawling up his neck. She was a great sister, except when she decided *he* needed to follow her advice. "Sarah..."

"When's the last time you dated?"

"July fourth. Took Beth Evers out to see the fireworks."

"You go out with her after that?"

"No, but..."

"Geeter. I don't want you to be alone. Burt and I are gettin' up there in age. Next year, we decided we want to try and have young ones, 'fore it's too late. I won't be able to take care of you all the time. You need a woman."

"I could probably hire one."

"Stop it and be serious. Ya' need someone to share your life. Please? Not for me, but for you?"

A random drip of sweat ran down his forehead. He removed the old John Deere hat and flung the perspiration off of it.

"Promise me you'll try, brother? I don't ask for much."

"Yeah right. Good thing I like you."

"That mean yes?"

"'Fore the end of the year, I'll see about datin', just to keep you happy."

"Promise?"

"Promise."

Sarah grasped him in a hug so hard he thought his eyes would bulge out of his head. "Just love you, that's all."

He kissed her cheek. "Love you, too." Geeter looked to heaven. *What did I get myself into now?*

Chapter 12

K elly closed the front door as she walked to her car, herding K.J. and the twins along. Davy was staying home with Mimi. Kelly shivered. *Temperature's dropping; winter's coming early this year.* Three small storms had left a covering of snow in the last couple of weeks, but forecasters were calling for the first significant snowstorm to blanket Chicago on Sunday afternoon.

Her phone pinged. *Todd.* Since that day in the parking garage, he had been the perfect gentleman. After getting the kids buckled in, she read his text. "Hey, Nurse Wonder Woman. Can't wait to see you at the café tomorrow morning. Should I order your normal, but maybe with pumpkin creamer in honor of the season?"

Her heart swelled. She replied, "You know me well, Dr. Doe. See you Saturday at ten."

Todd had taken it slow, rebuilding her trust. They had shared a few kisses, but that was only in the last month. Weekly café dates and a spattering of meals at a restaurant had her wanting more.

She closed her eyes as she remembered last Saturday's meeting for coffee.

Todd's smile was even more brilliant than ever. *"May I hold your hand, Kelly?"*

She nodded as she reached for him. The warmth of his hand sent shivers of desire up and down her spine. *When I hold your hand, I feel, well...*

His eyes were intense. *"I'd like to see more of you."*

She squeezed his hand. *"We have a date tomorrow night, silly."*

His eyes were like brown whirlpools in a chocolate jacuzzi, inviting and raising her body temperature. *"I know, but I was hoping we could move our relationship forward a little."*

Kelly's muscles tensed. Todd must have sensed her concern. *"Let me explain. I want to know you better. That means your children and family, too. They're important to you, so they'll be important to me as time goes by."*

Her mouth dropped open. The corner of Todd's eyes curled as he studied her face. *"I don't say it every day, but I feel it. I love you, Kelly. I hope you know that. I want to take all of you out to dinner."*

Her breath seemed to be coming fast. *"With four kids, that might be tough."*

He laughed. *"Hopefully, we'll do it many times over the years."*

The delight in his eyes confused her. *"Over the years?"*

"Yes, over the years. I'm hoping you and I have a long term, uh, relationship. Can we all go out to dinner?"

Kelly shook her head. *"I don't think that's a good idea."*

The disappointment in his face was so apparent. Kelly squeezed his hand tightly. She whispered, *"That wasn't a 'no'. I just don't think a restaurant is a good idea for the first time."*

His nose wrinkled as he watched her. *"Then what do you suggest?"*

Kelly took her time, taking a long sip of her mocha as she enjoyed the slight taste of chocolate. His anticipation was obvious, almost tangible enough to touch. It felt good to tease him. *"The first time you meet them should be at home. How 'bout dinner next Saturday night?"*

Melinda's voice brought her back to the present. "Mommy, can we get a snack at the grocery store?"

Tessa weighed in, "I get to pick."

"Not fair. You picked last time."

Kelly sighed, "Guys, if you're all three really good, I might let each of you pick something out. But you have to be good. Mommy's got to get groceries for tomorrow night. Someone special's coming over to meet you."

***

Saturday evening came much quicker than Kelly hoped. The whole house was filled with the enticing scents of homemade meatloaf, garlic mashed potatoes, gravy, and filling. Butterflies were again trying to carry her away. She was so nervous, knowing Todd would soon be there. She had explained to the kids that she was having a friend over, but wasn't sure how they would take it. Dr. Andrews arrived late, apologizing to everyone when Jeremy opened the door.

If Kelly was worried things would be awkward, her fears were quickly put to rest. Todd brought a rose for each of her girls, a small toy for K.J. and a snack for Davy. He wrapped his arms around Kelly, warming her from head to toe while his scent filled her heart. His lips were warm and wet when he kissed her cheek.

From the corner of her eye, she noted Kaitlin watching her with delight. Her sister had observed the kiss. She silently mouthed, "OMG! He's so hot!" Katie shot her two thumbs up.

Dinner was a blur, but a very happy one. The kids liked him. Her parents liked him. So did Jeremy and Kaitlin. She was touched when Todd read them a bedtime story after dinner. Kaitlin and Jeremy volunteered to take the kids upstairs for baths, offering to call Kelly when it was time for prayers and tuck-ins.

After the kids went to bed, Kelly led Todd to the swing on the front porch. It was freezing. Even in the dim light, his eyes sparkled. *I could look into your eyes forever.* "So, what do you think of my family, Dr. Doe?"

"Absolutely wonderful, just like you. So well behaved." The warmth of pride in her children swelled her chest. "I don't know how to say this. Tonight..." Her skin tingled as his fingers brushed against her cheek. "I love you, Kelly. I want, I want a life with you."

The tip of her nose tingled as she fought back her emotions. "I love you too, Todd."

Chapter 13

K elly wasn't surprised when the family decided to cancel the weekly Sunday meal. The snow had started in the morning, accumulating several inches by mid-afternoon. Kelly was coloring with the children in the downstairs playroom when she heard the doorbell ring.

Kaitlin's voice interrupted them. "Kelly, got a minute? Think you better come up here."

"Something wrong?"

"Just come up here, sis." She could swear Kaitlin was giggling.

Kelly walked up the stairs. Her mouth dropped open. Todd was standing there. "Hey, Kelly."

What's going on? "Hi, Todd. What are you doing here? Everything okay?"

At first Kelly was worried something was wrong, but Todd's spreading smile reassured her. The scent of his aftershave filled her senses. He reached for her hand.

"It is now. How spontaneous do you feel?"

"I-I dunno. What do you have in mind?"

"I thought a carriage ride in the snow might be fun."

Kelly's entire body warmed as she stared at him. "But, I... I... the kids, you know?"

Kaitlin whispered, "We got it, Kel."

She turned to her sister. "Sure you don't mind?"

"Go for it."

The crispness of the snow took Kelly's breath away. Snowflakes tickled her nose as he helped her to the SUV he had rented. "I, uh, you surprised me. I never expected this."

"I want you to get used to this. Kelly, I plan on spoiling you like this all the time."

"Why?"

He kissed her hand. Kelly's heart was about to jump out of her chest. "You should know by now. I love you."

***

Todd offered Kelly his hand after he opened the door. The delectable smell of pine trees and warm horses greeted her. She took the crook of his arm. He led her to the white open-topped carriage that awaited. A pair of red roan horses shivered in the brisk lake wind. Snowflakes mingled with the white hair flecked in their coats. Snowy feathered plumes towered above their majestic ears.

"My lady," the groomsman said before offering her his hand. Todd climbed into the carriage next to her. The groomsman covered them both with a bright red fleece blanket. Before climbing into the driver's seat, he uncorked a bottle of champagne and filled their flutes.

Kelly had no idea how long the ride was, or even where they travelled to. The only thing that mattered was the look in Todd's eyes when he smiled at her. *I know that look*. As if in response, he lowered his lips gently to her mouth. Kelly kissed him passionately in return. Todd's lips gently tugged at her bottom lip as he pulled away.

His laughter rang softly in her ears.

Kelly stuck out her bottom lip in a pout. "What's so funny?"

The depth of his gaze seemed to melt away her resistance. She was putty in his hands.

"This is." He removed a small ornate box wrapped with a red ribbon. Removing first the ribbon, then the lid, he revealed the most luscious looking chocolate covered strawberries. "I thought I ordered the sweetest dessert, but your kisses are sweeter." Once again, his lips touched hers.

Kelly was lost in the passion of the moment.

***

Todd opened the door to his house. He took her coat. The scent of nutmeg and cinnamon greeted Kelly as she hugged her arms to stave off the cold of the snowstorm raging outside. "What a magical afternoon. Maybe the most romantic of my life. The carriage ride was wonderful." *Because you were there.*

"I know we didn't talk about it, but I wanted you to see my home."

The large colonial was clean, spacious, and exquisitely decorated. *Too meticulous for a man's touch.* A strange thought entered her mind. "Who's your decorator?"

Todd swept his arm as if to showcase the house. "Not me. Hired a professional. Like it? What you think is important to me."

Kelly turned to gaze into those inviting pools of chocolate. "It is such a beautiful place. But why do you..." Todd's hand touched her arm. His eyes bored into her as if he were exploring her innermost being. This time, she had no urge to cover herself.

She let her sweater slip from her shoulders and reached for his cheeks. His five o'clock stubble was sharp. Kelly slowly pressed her lips to Todd's, his minty taste wearing down her last bit of resolve. When he moved his lips across her neck, heading toward her shoulder, all remaining resolve transformed into wild desire.

***

Kelly's mouth still tingled from Todd's kisses. Her heart had melted at his look of sadness, by the look of sorrow when she said she had to go. It was well after dark and by now, her children were no doubt in bed.

Todd guided the SUV into the driveway. Almost before she could unbuckle her belt, he was at her door, opening it, offering her his arm. The thirty or so steps to the front door seemed to take less than a nanosecond. The fire in his chocolate-colored eyes was still there, but on a slow burn. He whispered, "Good night. I wish it didn't have to end like this."

The feel of his lips against her fingertips as she traced their outline started to build her desire again. She stopped to hold his cheek. "End like what?"

"With you here and me going home to Walnut Meadows."

Kelly knew exactly what he meant. "Maybe this will help." Her strawberry-flavored gloss blended with the minty taste of his mouth as their lips met. Her hands pressed tightly against his ribs as she moved to hold him. Todd's arms caressed her shoulder and waist.

He suddenly pulled away. "If I don't leave now, I'm afraid I'll throw you over my shoulder and take you back home." Despite what he said, he pulled her tightly against him and kissed her with passion so deep, her knees trembled. As he let go and backed away, she grabbed the porch rail to avoid falling. "I'll see you this week." He blew her a kiss. "Love you, Kelly."

The SUV backed into the storm, Kelly's eyes following the tail lights until they left her vision. Her body ached for his touch, yet still tingled where his hands and lips had been.

Walking into the house, she wasn't really sure if her feet even touched the ground. The scent of freshly dried laundry greeted her. She gazed into the TV room. Kaitlin and Jeremy were folding clothes as she walked in.

Kaitlin's smile greeted her. "There's the prodigal sister. Of course you come back after everything's done. Have fun?"

Kelly replied almost breathlessly, "Wonderful."

Katie's smile changed from happy to inquisitive. Without taking her eyes from Kelly, she said to her husband. "Baby, I'm thirsty. Would you get me a diet Pepsi, please?"

"Be my honor. Want one, Kel?"

Kelly's eyes grew large as she watched Kaitlin's face. "No, I'm good." Jeremy walked to the kitchen.

Kaitlin skipped over, grasping Kelly's hands tightly. Her younger sister whispered, "You got lucky tonight, didn't you?"

Kelly's mouth went dry. "What? How can you tell, I mean, why would you think that?"

Katie's whole face smiled. "For starts, you look very, very relaxed. And there's this after lovemaking glow about you."

"That's all subjective. You have a dirty mind, sis."

Her sister was having such a hard time trying not to laugh. "Then, there's the physical evidence."

Kelly peered into Kaitlin's eyes. "What physical evidence?"

Kaitlin could barely contain herself. She held her stomach with one arm while her other hand pointed at Kelly. "Your shirt is on inside out!"

Kelly's cheeks heated intensely as she ran to her room.

Chapter 14

B y Tuesday evening, Kelly couldn't stand it any longer. A lack of appetite and general crankiness were the result of the romantic withdrawal, not being able to touch or kiss him. Kelly had worked the Monday afternoon and Tuesday day shifts. As always, Dr. Andrews made it a point to grace the sixth floor with his presence, but he had a shadow. A first-year med student tagged along on visits, so they couldn't talk.

After tucking the children in, Kelly decided to call him. They had texted frequently, but this was the first time she ever called. Her mouth was dry with anticipation, her heart ready to burst from her chest. She punched in his number.

A woman's voice answered, "Hello."

Kelly's spirits dropped. "I'm sorry, I must have the wrong number." Kelly was confused. This was the number she frequently texted.

Laughter. "Who were you trying to reach?"

"Dr. Andrews. Is this the right number?"

"Yes, it is. Let me get him. May I ask who is calling?"

"Of course, it's Kelly Jenkins."

"Oh, the nurse from Chicago General! Heard a lot about you. Let me get him for you."

It was a good three minutes before Todd came on. She could have sworn she heard a door close on the other end of the line. "What's up, Kelly? Something wrong?" He didn't sound happy to hear from her.

Her chin started to quiver. His demeanor struck her as odd. "No, not at all. I was missing you and wanted to ask if you would like to join the family at the hockey game on Sunday. My extended family will be there. Guess my timing was poor."

"No, no, not at all. My family came over for dinner. Just sitting down to eat. That was my, uh, sister. Can I call you later? It might be late."

Kelly shook her head. "That's okay, sorry for interrupting. No need to call me back."

"I want to. I just can't talk right now. That okay?"

"Sure."

His voice dropped to a whisper. "I love you. Talk to you soon. Bye."

***

Kelly groaned at the thought of the weekly Sunday dinner, held at Martina's this week. Kaitlin, her sweet sister Kaitlin, would no doubt blab to Martina about the costume malfunction. Martina would use her interrogation skills to delve into the matter. Despite knowing what was coming, Kelly's heart warmed at having such loving sisters. Even if they did circle like sharks at the first drop of blood.

Kelly tensed, knowing the teasing was about to begin when her oldest sister, Cassandra, skyped Martina. Martina sent it to the big screen TV in the home office. It was just the four sisters. Kelly knew pleasantries were over when Cassandra cleared her throat. "So, Kelly, Kaitlin tells me you have a new beau. Is that correct?"

Kelly's face turned hot as she realized it was only going to get worse. "Katie couldn't keep my secret, huh?"

Martina probed, as only an attorney could. "I understand that you even came home one night with your shirt inside out. Could you confirm or deny that allegation, Ms. Ballister?"

Kelly smiled. She could hold her own under Martina's cross-examination. Kelly took the offensive. "Ms. Davis, you know I no longer go by the last name of Ballister, but have once again assumed my maiden name of Jenkins. Could you please at least get the name of the accused right, counselor?"

Martina nodded. "Point taken, but could you please describe the events leading up to the incident for the jury?"

Kaitlin was laughing so hard she had to stop to catch her breath. Kelly smirked at her. Not that long ago, Kaitlin had been the one fielding hard questions from her sisters about Jeremy. "Go ahead, Kelly, and don't leave out the details on what time you got home last night."

Kelly's eyes lit up as she whipped around to face her younger sister. *I didn't think anyone noticed I snuck out.* "Kaitlin Elizabeth! I thought you were on my side in this!"

"Oh, I am. By the way, these fell out of your purse." Kaitlin held up a string of condom packets.

The heat rose in Kelly's cheeks. The good-natured teasing continued until it was time for the meal. Cassandra expressed her disappointment she wasn't with them in Chicago.

One of the Sunday family traditions was for each person to say what they were thankful for. When it was Kelly's turn, she decided to use the opportunity to take a jab at her sisters. She was smiling on the inside. "This week, Lord, I want to say how thankful I am for my family." She had to bite her cheek to keep from laughing. "I want to thank you for the kind, loving sisters I have, even if they do always stick their noses in my business. She's not here, but thanks for Cassandra and her eternal pessimism to keep me grounded."

Kelly's dad cleared his throat, his sign for her to behave. "Thank you for Martina, who treats every conversation like a cross-examination. And thank you for my baby sister Kaitlin, and her loose lips that couldn't keep bubble gum in her mouth if she tried. I love my family, Lord. Thank You for blessing me with them, as imperfect as they are."

Kaitlin quipped after Kelly's prayer, "And Lord, Kelly forgot someone. Thank you for bringing Todd into her life to brighten her days and add a certain sparkle to her nights!"

Their mother, Nora, cleared her throat loudly. "And we are also thankful for the love around this table, even when my daughters don't realize young ears are listening. I know it isn't humanly possible, but through your divine benevolence, Lord, please grant them the wisdom to know when they should be quiet. Amen! Now let's eat." The meal was delicious, spiced by the constant teasing. Not a single person was exempt, but Kelly received the lion's share.

The family arrived at the luxury box an hour before the opening faceoff. *Where are you, Todd? Better not stand me up.* Just before the puck drop, his frame filled the doorway. Kelly couldn't contain herself. She threw her arms around him, covering his face with kisses.

He whispered into her ear, "Missed you so much. I love you, Kelly."

The warmth of his embrace fueled the fires of desire. "I love you, too." Not another second was wasted watching the game. Every ounce of their being was spent in sweet conversation. Much too soon, they shared a knowing wink before uttering goodbye in the parking lot.

Back at the house, she wished away the minutes of bath time, prayers and fairy tale stories. It was all she could do to patiently wait until everyone went to bed. Half an hour later, Kelly snuck out. She was lucky she didn't get a speeding ticket, making it to Todd's place in record time. Todd greeted her at the door, wearing a plush terry cloth robe.

Their time together passed like a blink of an eye. Since Kelly had to work the next evening, she kissed him goodbye just after one in the morning. It took every ounce of strength to force herself into the car.

***

From the time she woke, happiness bubbled up, overflowing within her. In a very spontaneous mood, she stopped at a florist to purchase a bouquet of flowers. He was always so romantic. *I'll surprise you today.* The butterflies in her stomach must have called in reinforcements. Stopping at his practice, she walked to the counter carrying the bouquet. One of the patients in the waiting room coughed so harshly, Kelly had to turn to make sure they were okay. A very pretty nurse named Mandy appeared at the patient window.

Mandy smiled. "May I help you?"

Kelly's feet were barely touching the floor. *Can't wait to see you.* "Hi. Is Dr. Andrews available?"

"He's with a patient. May I help you?"

Kelly checked her watch. Plenty of time to get to work. "That's okay. I'll wait. Please tell him Kelly Jenkins is here."

Mandy's face brightened in recognition, "Kelly Jenkins, the nurse from Chicago General?" She offered her hand. "I'm so pleased to meet you."

What? Something nagged at Kelly's mind. "Thanks. How do you know who I am?"

Mandy laughed. "I'm sorry. We spoke on Tuesday. I answered Dr. Andrews' phone."

Kelly breathed a sigh of relief. "Oh, so you must be his sister. Pleased to meet you." Kelly grasped her hand.

Mandy quickly pulled her hand away. The girl's smile was quickly replaced with anger. "His sister? No! I'm his fiancée." She pointed to the bouquet in Kelly's arms. "What's this? You brought my fiancée flowers?" Chills ran down Kelly's spine. Before she had a chance to answer, Mandy drew a sharp breath. "He did it again! Why that little two-timing..."

At that moment in time, Todd escorted a patient into the waiting room. His deer-in-the-headlights look was apparent to Kelly. His mouth dropped open as he took in Kelly and Mandy, standing within three feet of each other. Todd's face turned ghostly white.

Pain radiated across her chest as Kelly realized what was happening. The idiot she was involved with was engaged to another woman!

Mandy was staring at Kelly. "You're the one. You made him cheat on me. That's why you're here!"

Kelly focused all her anger on Mandy as she growled, "I just brought him flowers to thank him for last night and, and to say goodbye, forever!" Kelly threw the bouquet on the counter. The white rose petals slowly floated to the floor, like autumn leaves, signifying the change of seasons. Kelly ran from the waiting room.

Chapter 15

G eeter drew in a deep breath. The crispness of the cold night air tickled his lungs. Orion had returned to his celestial hunting grounds, the glow of the Milky Way surrounding the constellation. He hopped up on the tailgate. For the first time in years, he was beginning to feel whole. Well, not whole. Connected was a better word. Returning to the life of a farmer, he had found a bond with his daddy. He missed his parents, though.

"Here ya go, Geeter." Burt handed his brother-in-law a hard cider from the six-pack.

"Thanks." The icy cold of the bottle made him shiver. "Well, all the crops is in. Looks like we did it."

They clinked the necks of their bottles together. "They say the first year's the hardest."

"Um-huh." Geeter drained the bottle with one long swig. The relaxed effect from the alcohol worked down his arms. "Somehow I think the hardest thing's in front of me yet."

"Yeah? What's that?"

"My promise to your wife."

"'Bout you findin' a woman?" Burt laughed.

Geeter twisted the top off a second bottle. "Yep."

"She knows you. Knows you just told her that to shut her mouth."

Geeter let a loud burp rip before scratching his chin. *Need to shave before I get serious.* "Gave Sarah my word. Gonna do it."

"Thought you didn't have a second date with the same girl in what, ten years?"

"Longer than that. But I got a secret weapon this time."

Burt raised an eyebrow. "Secret weapon? How many ciders you drank? Secret weapon my butt. What is it?"

He shivered. It was starting to get cold. *Soon time to go in.* "I'm getting help."

"From who?"

"My new romance coaches. Katie and Jeremy Roberts. They promised to help me get a woman."

Chapter 16

K elly's head was pounding. She had left an angry Mandy and an astonished Todd staring at each other. Reaching her car, she immediately called off work. She couldn't risk having Dr. Andrews show up while she was on her shift.

She drove around aimlessly before finding herself outside the old Sears Tower, where Jeremy and Kaitlin both worked. Taking the elevator to the twenty-third floor, she entered the office. Before she had a chance to speak with the receptionist, she saw Jeremy. He was standing in a back hallway, talking and laughing with a couple of co-workers.

Kelly suddenly felt dizzy. When his eyes met hers, his smile left and concern covered his face. Jeremy immediately dismissed the others and was quickly by her side. The room was spinning rapidly now. Jeremy swept her in his arms, heading back the hall. Just before Kelly lost consciousness, she heard him bark out an order, "Find my wife and have her meet me in my office, pronto."

Gentle pats against her cheek brought Kelly back to awareness. "Kel, wake up."

She pushed Kaitlin away. "Stop hitting me."

"Sorry. What's wrong?"

Her chest pounded. The words caught in her throat. "T-T-T-Todd used me, just like Ballister did. He, he's engaged! I can't go to work. He'll show up and I... I can't face him. I don't know what to do."

Kaitlin's arms comforted her. "Let's head home. We'll figure this out together."

***

Kelly was a jumble of emotions. Thank God her parents took the kids out for supper so they wouldn't be worried. Warmth and strength flowed into her as Kelly sat on the couch between her sister and brother-in-law, hands grasping hers. A soft knock on the front door startled her. She checked her watch. Five o'clock.

Jeremy left to answer the door. "Is Kelly here?" It was *him*. And the voice she'd loved, until today.

Kelly moved to where she could see the door. Jeremy didn't respond, preferring to stare him down while he balled his hands into fists. Todd couldn't see her, but he looked very uncomfortable under Jeremy's death ray stare. Jeremy's voice was icy. "Don't move." Then Jeremy slammed the door in his face.

The scent of Kaitlin's perfume filled her nose as her sister hugged her. "Who's at the door, Jeremy?"

"Andrews." He turned to look at Kelly. "Want me to send him away?"

That cheating... Her blood pressure rose as anger filled her mind. "No, I have a few choice words to say to him. I want the two of you there with me."

Jeremy opened the door, standing on Kelly's right while Kaitlin stood at her left. The good doctor looked very uncomfortable.

His voice squeaked, "Kelly, may I speak to you privately?"

Arms crossed, she glared at him. "No. Jeremy and Katie are staying right here. What do you want, you two-timing... snake?"

He gulped. "I need to explain. I love you. I was engaged, but was trying to find a way to break it off. And we did. We broke up this afternoon. Please forgive me. I can't live without you."

Just another lie. "I trusted you and you deceived me. To me, everything you said was a lie. You strung me along, telling me you were in love so we would have sex. You're scum. I'll never forgive you for what you did."

He quivered as he responded, "It wasn't like that at all."

A flash of light stunned her vision. *Need to calm down or I'll have a stroke.* She bit her lip, her voice calmer now. "Then how was it? If I hadn't caught you, would you have broken up with her?"

He was nodding his head rapidly. "Yes, yes I would have. I was trying to figure how to do it so I wouldn't hurt her. I care for her, but I love you, Kelly, you alone."

The pounding in her head surfaced again. "Lies, just lies. You're so full of crap, you stink. What exactly do you want?"

"This is going to be hard with us working together, and I..."

Kelly shook her head. "No, it won't be. I took a leave of absence. I won't return to the sixth floor and most likely not to Chicago General. This is the last time you'll ever see me. Anything else you want?"

He moved forward to reach for her, but Jeremy quickly stepped between them. "You will not touch her! Do I need to make it clearer?" Jeremy's face was flushed with anger. Todd backed up, but Jeremy took another menacing step toward him.

Jeremy's face was red, his lips white as he pressed them together. He kept balling his fists, inching closer and closer to Andrews. She could tell Jeremy scared the crap out of him. Andrews took another step backwards, looking over Jeremy's shoulder. "I didn't mean to deceive you. Please believe me. I had planned on marrying Mandy, but then you came along, and I... I fell in love with you. Head over heels."

Jeremy inched closer. Todd backed against the porch rail. "Please! I don't want to lose you. How can I make it right? I'll do anything to prove my love for you!"

Isn't that special? Kelly's face changed. She smiled sweetly as she stepped toward him. Kaitlin and Jeremy were mere inches away. "Well, there is one simple thing that can make everything right. Want to know what it is, honey?"

His face relaxed in relief. "Yes, yes, please tell me! I'll do anything you ask!"

"Here it comes." Kelly stepped forward as she raised her arm to slap him, but Jeremy grabbed it. Kelly yelled, "Let me go!"

The married couple both wrapped their arms around her. Kaitlin whispered, "He's not worth it."

Kelly exhaled sharply. "Fine. Let go. I won't hit him." The pair backed off. Kelly stared at him. "Not that you don't deserve it. Go to hell! Jeremy, get him off our property." Kelly turned her back, smartly stepping into the house, followed by Kaitlin.

Todd stood there, watching her retreat. Jeremy's voice snapped him to attention. "Leave now or I'll throw you into the street." Todd eyed Jeremy. "One, two..." Before Jeremy could reach three, Andrews was running for his car.

Jeremy yelled after him, "Leave her alone. God have mercy on your soul if you don't."

Todd sped off in his BMW.

Chapter 17

K elly stubbed her toe on the room service tray sitting in the hallway outside Kaitlin and Jeremy's hotel door. Kelly stooped to rub her foot. Kaitlin was so thoughtful, inviting her to visit New York with them. She missed her children, but Kaitlin had known she needed time away from them. This trip also got her away from Chicago. *And him!* Todd kept pestering her until Jeremy finally paid him a visit at his practice. That stopped Todd cold.

Jeremy opened the door to greet his sister-in-law with a big hug and a peck on the cheek. She smiled sadly. *I used to kiss everyone on the lips all the time.* Until the divorce.

Jeremy's laugh stopped her thoughts. "Katie's almost ready. You hungry? She wants to go to the diner across the street. I don't know about you, but I'm famished."

Kelly didn't understand. "We just ate. We had a late flight, but we did eat supper about eleven, didn't we?"

"Yeah, but that was yesterday."

"What gives with the room service tray in the hall?"

"We got the munchies last night."

Kaitlin came out of the bathroom, running to hug her sister. "Hungry, sis? I'm starved!"

Kelly gave them a strange look. "I don't understand. We ate at the same time, yet you two are starved. I'm not. What gives?" Her eyes got big. "Did you guys have any special activities going on last night that made you so hungry?" Both Jeremy and Kaitlin blushed as they glanced at one another. "At it again, weren't you?" They held hands, both sheepishly smiling at her.

Minutes later, they crossed 34th Street to the diner. The restaurant was packed with a long waiting line. Jeremy searched the dining room. Tapping his wife on the shoulder, he pointed. "There they are. I see Geeter."

The delectable scent of bacon was making Kelly's mouth water. "Geeter. That the guy you're helping?"

"Yep. There's his sister Sarah and her husband Burt, too." He had a mischievous look on his face. "Kelly, you up to having a little bit of fun?"

The scent of coffee now enticed Kelly. *Anything to distract me from my problems.* She had seen on TV the previous evening that her ex and the actress were divorcing. Not her problem, but it depressed her. A little bit of frivolity just might help. "What ya' got in mind?"

Jeremy quickly outlined a plan which made both sisters laugh. Kelly agreed but had to wait until she could keep a straight face.

Kelly walked over to the table where the man Jeremy called Geeter sat with his sister and her husband. The three appeared to be in deep discussion. Geeter's shoulders were slumped forward. His expression was one of sadness. *This might even do you some good.*

Kelly cleared her throat, waiting for him to notice. Geeter cast a quick glance at her before doing a double take. Kelly shot her prettiest smile at him. "Hey, Geeter! How's your morning going?"

Geeter shook his head, as if his mind had been in a fog. He stammered in his response, "Uh, it wasn't the best, but suddenly improved! Do I know you?" Kelly could almost see the wheels turning in his mind.

She shot him a puzzled look, "You do remember me, don't you? Shucks! You left something in my room last night." Sarah had been drinking her coffee, but suddenly spurted it out across the table into Burt's lap. Sarah's mouth dropped open.

Time stood still for Kelly as their eyes met. Okay, he wasn't all that attractive, but there was a depth to his gaze that brought warmth to her chest. His eyes were brown, like Todd's, but so different. His irises seemed to have sparkles in them. The warmth rapidly expanded from her chest to her limbs. Her soul was calm.

Geeter broke Kelly's trance. "What did I leave?"

What did Jeremy ask me to do? Oh, right. "A book and I'm pretty sure you were the one who left it."

The smile spreading across his face looked so appealing. The twinkle in his eyes grew merrier. "A book? What book?"

She smiled again, actively fighting off the urge to burst out in laughter. "Silly, you left a Bible. It said it was from Gideon... or was it the Gideons?" She put her forefinger to her cheek and reflected her gaze off into space.

Kelly expected he would laugh, but instead, his gaze intensified. "Couldn't have been me. If I had been with you, I never would have left!"

Kelly blushed. She thought this would be a funny moment, but instead...

Geeter stood, looking directly at Kelly. "Wait! I *do* know you. Well, sort of. You're Katie's sister, aren't you?"

After a sharp breath, it became hard to draw another one. "How could you possibly know that?"

When he smiled, his eyes twinkled even brighter. "You look just like her, only much prettier."

Kelly's cheeks were on fire. She was searching for something to say when Kaitlin's voice sounded from behind her.

"What? You think she's prettier than me? I thought we were buds." Kaitlin and Jeremy had walked over to the table. Kaitlin was smiling.

Geeter caught sight of Jeremy, his attention moving to his friend. They embraced, pounding each other's backs. Geeter pulled away, grabbing Kaitlin's hands. "Aw, Katie, I do think you're pretty, too. But you didn't tell me you were bringing an angel with you." While his words were to her sister, his eyes were on Kelly.

Jeremy laughed. "So good to see you. I see you've met my sister-in-law, Kelly. Sorry we pulled a trick on you."

Geeter again turned to glance at Kelly. "I don't mind at all." He turned his full attention to Kelly, extending his hand. "We ain't, I mean, we haven't been introduced. I'm, uh, my name is Gideon Beauregard Smith, but please call me Geeter."

The roughness of his hand in hers sent tingles up her arm. His handshake was firm, but she could tell he was holding back. His flannel shirt couldn't hide his bulging biceps. Geeter's gaze was intense, but so different than how Todd's had been. *Can this be real?* "Why do they call you Geeter?"

He smiled, "Well..."

Sarah laughed. "If he won't tell, I will. When Gideon was a wee little one, it poured down all summer. There were swarms and swarms of mosquitoes all around, but bubba couldn't say mosquito. It came out 'geeters,' so low and behold, the name stuck."

When they sat at the table, Kelly found herself to Kaitlin's left and Geeter's right. He held her chair for her. Her butterflies had come home to roost again.

Chapter 18

G eeter could barely eat anything at breakfast. This beautiful girl started a fire in him he hadn't felt in years. After breakfast, the party of six headed to Times Square to purchase theater tickets for an evening show. Geeter stared in shock when he and Kelly suggested the same show at the same exact time. After a quick discussion about how to spend the day, the women led the way to Macy's. Inside the massive store, the two couples headed in opposite directions.

"Seems like they abandoned us. Want to hang out?"

Kelly nibbled on her lip as she eyed him. Her mouth slowly broke into a smile. "I want to pick out a couple of souvenirs for my rug rats. That okay?"

He nodded. Just hanging out with this beautiful blonde was cool. Like a rose garden after a refreshing summer shower, her scent filled his nose. She had the most beautiful lips, covered with a slight glaze of bright red lipstick. *What do they feel like?* As soon as the thought entered his mind, Geeter chastised himself. This girl was something special, not one to lust over.

"I heard about you from Jeremy and Katie. They said they were helping you with something."

Geeter's cheeks turned red. "Yeah, you could say that."

She kept glancing at him as they shopped. "What are they helping you with?"

His mouth went dry. *This is gonna be embarrassing.* "My sister, well she wants me to... uh, you see, I, uh..."

Her eyes crinkled in a smile as she turned to him. "They already told me."

Oh no. "And you're teasing me. What did they tell ya?"

She laughed, suddenly reaching for his hand. "Katie said you've had trouble with women. So have I."

Geeter's eyes grew large.

"No, that didn't come out right. I've had trouble in the romance department. Did they tell you about me?"

Her hand was soft, and warm, and, well... perfect. "They didn't ever mention you." He touched her cheek softly. "Wish they would've."

She put her hand on his before looking deeply into his eyes. "My husband left me last year. Then there was this other jerk who..."

Kelly stopped when Geeter wiped the moisture from her cheek.

His voice was barely a whisper. "Damned idiots. You wanna talk about it?"

She had trouble fighting back a sob. "Only if you want to listen."

"I do. Hey, they have one of those fancy coffee stores here. Sarah's got me hooked on café mochas. Want one?"

The smile on her lips didn't hide her sorrow, but the look in her eyes said it all. His heart did a loop-de-loop after she squeezed his hand tightly. *I'm hooked.* "They're my favorite."

"Let's find a table."

They talked nonstop, as if they were old friends catching up on the past. But no old friend ever made him feel this way. Every nerve in his body was tingling.

He could only smile as her entire being captivated him, drawing him to her like a magnet attracts steel. The coffee cups had long since been drained.

Kelly studied his eyes. "May I ask a question?"

"'Course."

"Did you spike my mocha?"

Laughter bubbled from inside him like a spring. "Heck no. Why would you even think that?"

"Dunno. Talking with you, I feel, uh, tipsy inside." Kelly's laughter drifted toward him like the peals of distant church bells on the breeze. "Not trying to get me drunk, are you?"

Geeter reached across the table, his calloused hands touching her ivory skin. "Hell no. Never'd want to change you. You're perfect just the way you are."

Kelly turned her hands over, moving her fingers against his palms. She lowered her eyes. To Geeter, it seemed like a rainstorm ruining a sunny day. "Did I do something wrong?"

"No, absolutely not. Just lost in thought." She raised her chin slightly so their eyes connected. "Geeter..."

"There you are!" Sarah's voice broke the trance. "We were thinking about sendin' out a search party for y'all."

Kelly quickly pulled her hands from his.

Kaitlin toted a small bag. Jeremy stood beside her with several more. "You guys ready to move on? We were thinking about heading to the Empire State building. Jeremy's going to run the bags back to the hotel. Why don't you tag along with him, Geeter?"

No, I want to stay with your sister. He chanced a glance at Kelly. She smiled sadly and looked away. "'Kay. L.T. and I'll run 'em back. Meet y'all in a jiffy." As they walked off, he looked over his shoulder. Kelly was watching. With a disappointed smile, she waved goodbye.

Geeter didn't want to go, but he did. As soon as they walked out of the hotel lobby, he flagged down a taxi.

Jeremy frowned. "Are you serious? A cab? We can walk there in a couple of minutes."

"Sorry, L.T. Just anxious, that's all."

They climbed in the taxi. Jeremy studied him as the blocks slid by. His former commander's voice softly resonated. "Geeter?"

"What?"

"Careful. That's my sister-in-law. She's a little tender."

"Understood. But remember, you introduced us." Before Jeremy could respond, Geeter paid the fare and was out of the door.

It took a few minutes to catch up with the girls. As they stood in line, Jeremy explained one of the wishes on Kaitlin's bucket list was to be kissed at the top of the building. The line was long and slow moving, but no one minded. They passed the time with gentle joking and shared stories. It was almost noon before they reached the observation deck.

Geeter's belly felt funny as they rode the elevator to the top. Heights never scared him. *Wonder what's going on in there?*

The doors opened and they flowed out to the walkway, the sights of New York City below them. Almost immediately, Jeremy wrapped his arms around his wife to share several long, romantic kisses. Sarah and Burt did the same.

Geeter and Kelly walked around the deck, looking out at the city. It was his first time in New York, but the panorama below didn't interest him at all compared to the beautiful girl at his side. The sunlight caressing her hair set her locks ablaze in a golden hue. Geeter had never felt the nervous energy running down his limbs.

Kaitlin finally came over to tell them they were going to head back down in five minutes.

Kelly turned to face Geeter, a look he didn't quite understand on her face. *Fear or... longing?*

The words leaving his lips surprised him. "Do you believe in fate?" His heart skipped a beat from the intensity of her gaze.

"No, but I believe God has a master plan for everything. Why do you ask?"

"I was just thinking, what's the possibility you and me would, would ever meet? I was thinking it was fate, but maybe you're right. Maybe God had this planned."

Kelly smiled at him. "Maybe He did." She eyed him as if puzzled. "Want to ask me something?"

Miss this, and you'll always regret it. He could feel the heat flash in his cheeks. "I was wondering, w-would y-you like a kiss up here?" Chills ran up his spine. "Maybe I'm being a little too forward, Kelly. If you say no, I understand. I really do."

Her eyes fluttered back and forth between his, reminding him of a hummingbird flitting from flower to flower. Her voice was barely above a whisper. "I'd be honored."

Geeter's entire body tingled as he gently wrapped her in his arms. Leaning in, he softly gave her a quick peck on the lips.

She pushed him away, eyes smoldering. "That wasn't a proper kiss!" He almost fainted when she grabbed him tightly. Her soft, wet lips pressed firmly against his, remaining there for several seconds. She pulled away, her tongue wiping her upper lip. "Now that's better."

I could die a happy man right now. He gently pulled her toward him, pressing his lips delightfully against hers again. A warm, captivating feeling surrounded him. It took a few seconds to realize it was her arms.

All too soon, she pulled away, a soft moan coming forth from her lips. Kelly pressed her cheek to his. "You should be giving lessons, not getting them."

Geeter started to giggle, but Kelly went on the offensive, her soft lips meeting his again. Desire to hold this woman tighter grew in him, eclipsing the height of any skyscraper.

They had barely broken apart when he overheard Kaitlin whisper in Kelly's ear, "Seems the shoe's on the other foot now."

Kelly blushed before breaking out in such an infectious laugh that Geeter joined in. Riding the elevator back to street level, she reached for his hand. They ignored the stares of the two couples watching them in disbelief.

***

Kelly's head was spinning. This had to be a dream, a wonderful dream. She couldn't believe how much fun she was having with a man she'd met just hours ago! They fit together so naturally. Their conversation was nonstop, as if they couldn't share fast enough.

After being seated at Bubba Gump's restaurant, the waitress came over. "Do you like trivia? Forrest Gump said he and Jenny went together like what vegetables?"

At the same time, Kelly and Getter hollered, "Peas and carrots." A shared laugh. For the entire meal, the other two couples sat back, watching Kelly and Geeter tease each other about the movie.

Kelly scraped the last molecules of ice cream from her dish, the crisscross pattern glistening in the light. She turned to him. "You really single?"

The look in his eyes just about brought her to her knees. "I was wondering the same thing about you. Never met any woman like you, so perfect. I should be asking if you're married or engaged." He leaned toward her but didn't kiss her. She wished he would. "By the way, yes."

Yes, what? "Come again?"

"Single."

Kelly's shoulders relaxed. *Me, too.* "Today's been absolutely magical."

Geeter gently brushed her bangs from her eyes. "Your day's about to get better."

What? "I don't understand."

"Trust me, okay?"

Warm, tingly feelings ran through her chest. "I do trust you, totally."

Twenty minutes later, he helped her to her feet. "I haven't skated in years. I'm afraid I might fall."

Geeter's smile bored through her body into her heart. "I won't let that happen. Haven't ice skated for years, but I can roller skate with the best of 'em."

They skated side by side. With his arm wrapped around her waist, she could conquer the world. *Never imagined skating could be so romantic.* Geeter removed his arm, holding her hand tightly. He spiraled them toward the center of the ice. His arms embraced her, raising her body temperature so high, she was surprised the ice didn't melt beneath her skates.

"Kelly. Spending today with you has been like spending a day with a princess. There's no words I could ever think of that could say what I'm feeling in my heart."

Kiss me. He leaned in until his forehead touched hers. The warmth of his body was making her dizzy. She ran her fingers through his hair. *Kiss me!* She raised her lips, anticipating contact, but the gentle touch drove her to the edge of her control. Her heart urged her to do more than kiss him.

"I hope you realize you're perfect in my eyes."

"Geeter, I, uh..."

He eased away from her, again placing his arm around her waist as they slowly skated away. "I know, Kelly."

She chanced a glance at his face. His eyes sparkled in the dimming lights as dusk overtook them. *Most romantic moment of my life.*

After dinner, they met the other two couples at the theater to see *Mamma Mia*. Kelly squeezed his hand. "I loved ABBA's music. What about you?"

His laughter tickled her imagination. "My favorite group of all time."

They held hands, singing along loudly during the performance... so loudly in fact that Sarah yelled at them to be quiet so other guests could hear the music!

Kelly's heart was dancing, and she pinched herself. *Is this real or just a dream?* As if in response, Geeter reached over to gently kiss her. This was real. *Is this what love feels like?*

Chapter 19

H er soft terry robe enveloped her like a fleece blanket, covering her silky traditional pajamas.

Kelly knocked and Kaitlin immediately opened the door. "We thought you'd drop by." The sound of the shower running told her where Jeremy was.

You did? "Why'd you think that?"

Kaitlin gave her an odd smile. "Pretty extraordinary day for you, wasn't it?"

The day had been perfect, the stuff of dreams. "Yeah, it was." Kelly could still feel his hand in hers, the warmth of his lips gently pressing against hers.

"Kel?"

She opened her eyes. Kaitlin was closely watching her.

"What?"

"I'm worried about you. Be careful."

"What? Today was the most magical day of my life."

"Only because you're on the rebound from Todd. You're going to get hurt. What you're feeling isn't real."

Kelly's jaw clenched. "Don't use that psychological bullcrap on me, Kaitlin Elizabeth. I'm the master of my own feelings. I'm quite capable of knowing what I feel."

"I wasn't trying to put you down, but consider this. Three months ago, would you have given Geeter a second look?"

86

"What do you mean?"

"A, he's not attractive. B, he's not your equal intellectually. C..."

"Stop. Don't you dare try to control me. I didn't criticize you when you fell in love with a soldier, someone who certainly wasn't your equal in any way."

Jeremy's voice startled her. "You're right. I wasn't your sister's equal, but I was somewhat close. Geeter isn't. Not close by any stretch of the imagination. Just a simple farm boy."

Her nostrils flared. *What gives you the right?* "All right, Mr. Know-it-all. Tell me how you really feel."

He shared a look with Kaitlin before walking close to take Kelly's hand. "To be blunt, Geeter's not good enough for you."

The sound of voices passing in the hallway distracted her. A very odd thought nagged at her mind. *No. They wouldn't do that.* "Did your invitation for me to tag along have anything to do with you coaching him on how to handle women?"

Jeremy ripped his hand from hers. "No!"

"You sure?" She turned to her sister, voice softer. "And you. You're my best friend. All my life, I supported you. Wanted you to be happy. It's my turn now. Aren't I entitled to a little happiness, too? And I am happy. Please don't spoil it for me."

Tears welled in Kaitlin's eyes. "You're right. I didn't realize what I was doing. Sorry, Kel." Kaitlin wrapped her arms around her big sister.

Jeremy shook his head, walking to the bedroom where he closed the door and turned on the TV.

Kaitlin wiped her cheeks. "Sit. Tell me about your day, the things I don't know."

Kelly's eyes were still smoldering. "No. I think I'll keep it to myself. After all, he isn't my equal."

"Okay. I get it. How about if I asked for your forgiveness. Will you tell me then?"

"What's it worth to you?"

Kaitlin smiled. "Name your price."

***

The night ended way too soon for Geeter. The Chattanooga crowd was staying in the garment district while the Chicagoans were staying above Grand Central Station. Geeter said good night to Sarah and Burt when they left the theater. It felt so natural to be with Kelly when he escorted her to her room. The good night kiss was heavenly. Walking back to his hotel, he breathed in the cold, crisp winter air to clear his mind. Walking past the ice rink in Bryant Park, a beautiful thought filled his mind.

Geeter navigated the now empty streets on the way back to Grand Central. A few vendors were still open, and Geeter bought something special. *This is crazy, this is crazy.* While his mind spoke, his heart refused to listen. When he got off the elevator at Kelly's floor, his heart was at the pit of his stomach.

His head was spinning as he knocked on her door, but there was no answer. *Is this the right room?* He had to see her again, tonight. *Right floor?* No answer. Maybe Kelly was over in Jeremy and Kaitlin's hotel room. He dialed Jeremy's cell.

Kaitlin answered Jeremy's phone on the third ring, "Hello?"

"Uh, Katie, hi. This is, um, Geeter. How are you?"

Kaitlin laughed. "I'm fine, Geeter, and how are you?"

He was so nervous, not knowing exactly what to say. "I'm good, uh, this is Geeter." He winced as soon as the words left his lips.

He had to move the phone away from his ear, due to Kaitlin's loud laughter. "I think we have established the fact that you truly and absolutely are the one and only Geeter. Can I help you with something, or do you want to speak with Jeremy?"

"Uh, no. I don't want to bother him. Look. Maybe you can help me. I just wanted to ask, is Kelly with you?"

She acted shocked. "Why yes, she is! Would you like to speak with her?"

"Well no, I mean yes. I mean, uh, what room are you in? I have something I want to give her."

Kaitlin's laughter increased before she hung up. Three doors down, a door opened. Kaitlin waved. "She's in here. Come join the party."

Warmth flowed upwards as she smiled at him. Kelly had changed clothes and was now sporting the loveliest set of silk pajamas he'd ever seen. *Man, she's gorgeous.*

Her laughter sounded like a summer breeze rippling through a cornfield. "Looking for me?"

He hadn't thought this through very well.

Geeter stuttered as he replied, "Uh, y-y-yes, I was. I, uh, b-b-bought you something." He pulled the bouquet out from behind his back.

Kelly's face lit up as soon as she saw the flowers. Her eyes glistened.

"I b-b-brought you flowers to th-th-thank you for today."

Much to his surprise, she bounded across the room to hug him. He relaxed, having never felt better. Pulling back, she gazed into his eyes briefly before gently giving him a warm and wet kiss. Kaitlin howled with laughter, but Geeter ignored her and devoted all of his attention to Kelly.

Kaitlin started counting, "One, two, three, four..."

Kelly pulled away from the embrace but didn't face her sister. Laughing, she said, "Grow up, Katie!" Grabbing Geeter's arm, she pulled him into the hallway. Closing the door behind her, she stopped laughing and studied him seriously. "Thank you. The flowers are lovely. And today has been a dream." She pressed her lips against his again. Not even the taste of the sweetest wine ever could compare to her kisses.

Her next kiss made the room spin. He held her until it passed. "Would you have breakfast with me again tomorrow?"

Kelly placed her lips against his ear, those luscious lips softly touching his earlobe. "You mean just us... or everyone?"

"I don't care. I really need, I mean, I want to see you again."

Her smile changed from one of total joy to a devilish smile. "Hmm, I see. How about eight, same diner where we first met?" She winked, whispering in a soft and conspiratorial tone, "We better have everyone join us, or they might suspect something is going on."

Something good is going on. His lips caressed hers, tasting her sweetness. Reluctantly, he pulled away.

After knocking on Jeremy's door, he made sure Kelly got inside safely. His feet didn't seem to touch the carpet on the way down to the street level.

Chapter 20

G eeter couldn't sleep at all that night. Kelly's face danced through his mind. He woke Burt and Sarah at five to make sure they wouldn't be late. They arrived an hour early and spent the time just sitting in the lobby of Kelly's hotel.

Geeter disappeared for a while before returning with a new outfit and a large paper bag.

As soon as Kelly stepped out of the elevator, Geeter hurried to greet her. He handed her the second bouquet of flowers. "You really look absolutely enchanting this morning."

Kelly didn't say much as she checked out his clothes. Yesterday, he'd worn an old flannel shirt and jeans. But this morning, he was dressed in khaki Dockers and a neatly pressed chambray shirt, mint green. He hoped she liked his new clothes.

Sarah and Kaitlin poked fun at Geeter and the way he acted. He held the outside door of the restaurant open for Kelly, almost letting it slam in Burt's face when he ran to hold the inner door for her. In the dining room, he held her chair, took her coat, and complimented her so many times even he lost count.

Sarah pointed at Kaitlin and Jeremy as she dropped into her Southern drawl, "I know the two of y'all are to blame for what's goin' on here. I don't know what ya did with my brother, but I'd like to have him back at the end of the trip. I can't put up with him actin' like this all the time!"

Jeremy slowly commented, "We didn't do anything with him, but the change is rather amazing, isn't it?"

Kaitlin quipped, "It seems he joined the human race. You should have heard him last night when he called. He told me twice what his name was."

They continued to poke fun. He was trying to be as nice as possible, but their comments hurt. Of course he realized a woman as terrific as Kelly was out of his league, but he really cared for her. He had to try. He wanted to impress her.

Kelly cleared her throat loudly, startling everyone. "That's enough." Her serious tone got everyone's attention. "I think Geeter is just wonderful, and if you keep it up, we'll go our way, and you can go yours. Take that as a threat, warning, or promise, I don't care, but knock it off. The smart comments stop now, do you understand?"

Kaitlin laughed, "But it's so comical, Kelly, you..."

"I'm serious, Kaitlin Elizabeth Roberts. Either all of you knock it off immediately, or the next time you'll see me will be on the airplane."

Silence ensued around the table.

Kelly turned to Geeter, "And that, my friend, is how you handle our families." She gave them another very evil look before turning her gaze to Geeter, politely asking, "Honey, you mind ordering breakfast for me while I use the powder room?"

As soon as she was out of earshot, Sarah whispered in disbelief, "Did she just call him 'honey'?"

But Kaitlin wasn't laughing, "Kelly's not joking. We better back off a little." She turned to Geeter with a smile and a wink, "Sorry, Geeter. We all apologize."

Geeter smiled shyly, confessing, "I'm sorry. I'm not very good at this. Kaitlin, your sister is something very special. I'm trying so hard to impress her."

Kaitlin's smile left her face as she touched his hand. "Let me give you some advice, Geeter. Be genuine, be yourself. Everyone can see how hard you're trying, but if you come across as something you're not, Kelly will pick up on it, and it'll all be over."

Geeter hung his head. "I get it."

Kaitlin frowned. "We just care about her. She likes you, but her ex and that idiot doctor hurt her with their lies. That wound is still open and very painful for her." Her smile returned. "Despite the fact we're picking on you, we..." she shot Jeremy an evil look, "...well... at least I'm rooting for you."

Geeter sighed. *Katie said Kelly liked me!* It had been so long since he cared for someone. But something nagged at him. She'd asked him to order breakfast, but he couldn't remember what she'd eaten yesterday. Oh, he knew what shoes, dress, and coat she had worn. He even remembered her scent, but food? No way.

Panic rose in his chest as Kelly worked her way back from the restroom. He turned to Jeremy. "What should I order for her?" Jeremy looked at him without emotion, Geeter begged, "Please L.T., I'll be forever in your debt. Please help me!"

Kaitlin whispered sharply, "Jeremy Allen Roberts!"

It was too late. Kelly had returned. Geeter stood up to push in her chair. With her back to him, he motioned to the group to help him. With a look of disdain, Jeremy 'accidentally' knocked over the salt and pepper shakers. Geeter got the hint and leaned down to help pick them up.

Jeremy mumbled, "Two eggs, sunny-side up, bacon crisp but not burned, English muffin with real butter, orange juice, and coffee with two sugars but no cream."

The waitress returned to take their order. Kelly smiled brightly when Geeter ordered breakfast exactly the way she liked it. She rewarded him with a kiss on his cheek and a prolonged squeeze of his hand.

The morning was spent at the new Freedom Tower and memorial museum. This was hallowed ground for both Geeter and Jeremy. Their lives had been forever changed by the attacks that took down the World Trade Center. Geeter couldn't help it. There was sorrow in his eyes as he remembered that horrible day—the day that changed his life. Kelly must have sensed it. She gave him a long and tight hug.

The spicy food from Chinatown burned going down, but her kisses soothed him. After lunch, they took the boat to see Lady Liberty on her little island in the harbor. As they viewed New York's skyline, Geeter held Kelly, her head on his shoulder. Each moment he was with her seemed to top the previous.

After dinner, Kelly and Geeter paired off to end the evening by themselves, slowly walking to the center of the city. Kelly turned to him, the depth of her eyes making him sigh. "The lights in Times Square are beautiful. Thank you for bringing me here."

Every cell in his body felt good. "You think these lights are something, you should see the stars from my farm. You can see the whole Milky Way." A few snowflakes fell from the sky, big and fluffy. He brushed one from her hair. "I hope you'll come visit me sometime."

Kelly eyes were sparkling. "In the spring?" Her eyes were prettier than the brightest star in the sky.

Her smile turned him on. He kissed her, slow and deep. "I'd love that. Your children would love it there, too. Nothing like a farm for little ones to play on. But I have to be honest, I don't think I can wait until spring to see you."

She drew in close, squeezing his hand. "Do you have plans for Christmas?"

Chapter 21

K elly entwined her arm through his as they walked past Radio City Music Hall. Her mind was a jumble of emotions. Today was the last full day in New York and it had passed so quickly. She and Geeter spent the day together, just the two of them. The closeness of walking, talking and shopping was like the buzz from drinking a tall glass of wine. They'd had dinner at the Rainbow Room in the GE building, mesmerized by the changing hues of Christmas colors displayed on the Empire State building, charmed by the sparkling eyes and warm hands of the man sitting across from her. Absolutely perfect.

Geeter stiffened and stopped. She followed his gaze to the tree at Rockefeller Plaza. The lights were shining through the snowy night like a lighthouse on a foggy evening. The large snowflakes drifting down reminded her of fireflies.

Geeter turned to her. "That's the second most beautiful sight I've ever seen. Thanks for sharing it with me."

Just gazing into those eyes brought a full smile to her face. "Second? What's first?"

His response was immediate. "You."

Kelly had to bite her lips together to keep her sigh inside. Smiling into her eyes, Geeter wrapped his arms around her waist. Kelly snuggled deep in his embrace before she found his lips.

Warmth flowed through her from head to toe. Something about Geeter told her she could trust him, totally. *Why do I feel so comfortable with him?* It wasn't infatuation. His face wasn't attractive, but his genuineness and kind personality had her more turned on than Todd's good looks ever had.

She pulled from the embrace to draw a breath. Geeter was funny, caring and gentle. But Kaitlin's words haunted her. *Am I on the rebound or is this real?*

Under the tree, Geeter moved his lips gently against her neck, softly kissing her skin. She tilted her head to the side to give him better access. She held his hands as he nuzzled her neck. Excitement grew by leaps and bounds.

His stubble caught in her hair as he whispered in her ear, "I'm not good with words, but I never dreamed I could feel this way about a woman." He spun her around to face him. "Kelly Jenkins. You're perfect and I, I... I'm lost to say anything better. You were right. God did intend for us to meet."

She turned quickly because she didn't want him to see her eyes filling. Kelly snuggled her back against his chest. *We go our separate ways tomorrow.* She squeezed his hands, only to have him squeeze back. His lips again roamed down her neck. She leaned her head back against his shoulder, snowflakes tickling her face as if butterflies were caressing her, while Geeter's lips running up and down her neck mesmerized her.

Suddenly, she knew exactly what she wanted. Kelly turned to him, again gently kissing his lips. In a voice barely louder than a whisper, she said, "I want to go back to my hotel room now."

He looked as if he'd been struck by a car. "No, please. We only have a short period of time. Don't let the night end so soon."

Her arms were still wrapped around him. "It won't."

***

Morning broke bright and clear, but the tall buildings held back the sun from the street. An errant ray of sun penetrated the curtains, lighting up the dust particles dancing in the air. She shifted her focus to the man sleeping in her bed. Tears stung her eyes. She'd lost so much over the past twelve months. Where would she be in another twelve? Would she be happy?

Geeter stirred in his sleep. Could she find happiness with him? Had it only been three days since they met? The time together had been wonderful, but she wasn't sure if she had the courage to find out. In a short while, they would board separate planes to different cities.

Geeter's eyes opened, and he smiled at her. She returned his gesture, hoping her sadness didn't show through.

Geeter eased onto one elbow. "Morning, beautiful." He searched her face, and his smile disappeared. "I do something wrong?"

Kelly shook her head.

"You regret sleeping with me?"

Kelly bit her lips, but took a few seconds before shaking her head.

"Please talk to me."

Kelly brushed the red hair from his eyes. With a crooked smile, she said, "Good morning, sport. How are you feeling today?"

"What's happening in your pretty little head?"

Her eyes were scratchy again. Her smile couldn't cover her wounds. His look moved her heart. *Can't lie to him.* She barely nodded. "Just thinking about everything that transpired in the last year. A little sad about it, that's all."

Geeter looked away and frowned. *Maybe she's sorry we made love.*

She reached for his hand, the touch of his calluses firm against her fingers. "Why the frown? Sorry you spent last night with *me*?"

"No, I'm not. But I'm afraid you are." He ran his fingers through his hair. "I believe I know how this goes. I'll never hear from you again when I leave this room. I thought we stumbled onto something wonderful. But if I thought it would come to this, I wouldn't have stayed the night."

Kelly's heart melted.

He was fighting back emotion.

"Never met anyone like you. You're so special. If I hurt you, I didn't mean to. Should've known you're too much of a reach for someone like me."

His words choked her. She had to clear her throat. "You said an awful lot there. First, I wanted last night. Second, I want to continue what we started here. It's going to be hard, but not impossible." She bent to kiss his lips. "I really like you, Geeter. You're funny and you warm my heart."

"I really like you, too."

"What happened last night never happened before. It's just the chemistry between us was so special, I couldn't help myself."

"Last night was magical, Kelly."

She placed her forefinger against his lips. "Yes, it was. Finally, you didn't hurt me, unless this is your way of dumping me."

The sparkle returned to his eyes. "I would never dump you."

She touched his nose. "Good." She studied his eyes. "What did you mean, I was a reach for you?"

He frowned, looking extremely uncomfortable. "Kelly, you're so classy. And me? I'm just some dumb redneck guy who doesn't feel worthy enough to hold your hand."

Her heart again flooded with warmth. She brushed his cheek with her fingers. "Thank you, but I don't see it that way. You're genuine and kind; any woman would be lucky to have you." She lowered her lips to his. "Now, we're both going home today, so let's come up with a plan."

Chapter 22

K elly was reflective as they drove home from the airport, thinking of Geeter. The emptiness in her heart was like someone had vacuumed out all the good feelings. She'd known him for such a short time, but she missed him. The sudden ringing of her cell brought her back to the present.

She didn't recognize the number. "Hello?"

"Kelly, it's Geeter. I miss you. How was your flight?"

Her throat closed, making it hard for words to come out. "Pretty bumpy. Missed you, too. It's only been a few days, but I kind of got used to you being around. It hurts inside, you not being with me."

"I know. Miss you, too. Whole flight, all I could think about was your smile."

Kelly was riding in the backseat of Jeremy's truck. Kaitlin was watching her in the mirror. She remembered her sister had gone through this when Jeremy had been injured and she'd had sent him back to Chicago. Kaitlin and Jeremy had worked through that tough time. Would she and Geeter be able to do the same?

Kelly turned from her sister's gaze, blushing as she replied, "That's sweet. I miss your voice and how you make me laugh. Did you think about coming to Chicago for Christmas?"

Her heart tumbled when she heard his sad sigh. "I did. Talked with Sarah and Burt. Gonna be a bad Christmas for Sarah. Was always Mom's favorite time of year. I want to be with you, but I need to be with her. Maybe New Year's?"

Though she didn't say it, his answer depressed her. "I'd really like that. Maybe we could Skype or FaceTime each other. Would that be okay?"

"Sure! I'll get someone to show me how to use it. Mind if I text you?"

"That would be nice. And Geeter?"

"Yeah?"

Kelly lowered her voice to a whisper. "I really care for you. Don't forget about me."

"That'll never happen, I promise. And just so you know, I really, really care for you, too. Have a good night."

"You too. Bye."

Kelly closed her eyes to stem the tears.

"You okay, Kel?"

Kelly nodded but didn't say anything. A lonely tear tracked down her face.

"Kelly, the whole distance-thing can be hard. It was rough on us, but we got past it."

Kelly missed Geeter so much. Suppose she never saw him again? "I remember, but there wasn't any doubt the two of you would be together forever. I really like Geeter, but I'm afraid the distance is going to be too much."

Kaitlin had turned to face Kelly. "Our relationship wasn't guaranteed. We worked hard for it, but it worked out."

Kelly wasn't really listening. "And suppose you're right? What if my feelings are so strong because I'm on the rebound? You're lucky, sis. You found the love of your life. I don't have that."

Kaitlin reached for her sister's hand. "Not yet, but remember this. Everything happens for a reason. Looking back later in life, everything will be revealed. You've gone through hell. Just hang in there and let things happen naturally."

"You don't understand."

"Yes, I do. If Geeter is the one God wants you to be with, nothing, not time nor distance nor anything else will keep you apart. If he isn't, God will send someone very special to you. I believe in my heart you weren't meant to go through life alone. I'll always love you, and I'll be here for you, just like you were always there for me."

Kelly smiled. "I love you, too, and thanks. I invited him up for the holiday, but he's staying there because Christmas is going to be hard for Sarah, you know, with losing their parents and everything. He said he might be able to make it up after Christmas, but I wish he were here now."

Kaitlin's smile lifted her heart. "There's always room at our house for New Year's." Kaitlin turned to Jeremy. "Isn't that right, honey?"

Jeremy was silent.

Kaitlin jabbed him in the ribs. "Isn't that right, Jeremy Allen?"

"Sure, why not? Geeter and I celebrated two New Year's Eves together in Iraq, but this time, we won't have to share a bunker or be watchful for snipers."

"Thank you. You two are the best."

Kaitlin gave Jeremy the evil eye. "Well, we're working on it."

Chapter 23

As Christmas approached, life became hectic for Kelly. She resigned from Chicago General to take a position on the evening shift at a nursing home. Kelly hated the evening shift because she missed so much time with her children, so she hoped to find a different job with better hours after the holidays.

When Kelly opened the front door, the scent of pine and cinnamon gently greeted her. After dropping her keys in the bowl on the stand, she kicked off her shoes. The flickering light from the gas fireplace was so inviting. A movement caught her attention—Kaitlin. Katie often waited up to greet her when she got home.

Kaitlin's face had a tired smile. "Hey, Kel. Mom and the kids baked cookies. Brought us a plate to share and a cup of hot chocolate. How was your night?"

The stuffed chair was so comfortable. Kelly snuggled in as her sister handed her the mug. It had whipped cream with crumbled peppermint on top. "Pretty quiet, which was good. Short staffed, which appears to be normal there. How were the kids?"

Kaitlin passed the plate of chocolate chip cookies. "Heated them in the microwave, so they might be a little warm. The kids? Well, K.J. read *Hop on Pop* out loud by himself tonight. The twins were fashionistas. See how they did Jeremy's hair?" Katie passed her iPhone to Kelly. "Davy was cranky. Mom thinks he's cutting teeth."

The taste of the warm gooey cookie brought back happy memories of Kelly's youth. *Will the memories my kids have be happy?* She fought back a tear. "I hate this shift. Seems like life's passing me by."

"I'm sure it's only temporary. Talk to Geeter today?"

The fluffiness of the whipped cream tickled her upper lip as she took a sip. "Yeah."

"And?"

Kelly picked up and studied the heavy, ugly vase sitting on the coffee table. "I thought you hated this vase. Why do you keep it?"

"Because Cassie gave it to me for my birthday when I was six. I hate that thing."

"It's ugly. Throw it away."

"My conscience won't let me. Now, what's happening with Geeter?"

"I don't know. I really like him, but..."

Kaitlin leaned over from her chair to grab another cookie. "But what?"

Kelly put down her mug and moved to the ottoman so she could look directly at her sister. "Is there something wrong with me?"

Kaitlyn was dipping the cookie in her hot chocolate. "Whatcha mean?"

"First, Ballister dumps me. Then Todd deceives me. And Geeter..."

"What did Geeter do?"

"It's what he didn't do."

Kaitlin raised an eyebrow while she stuffed her moist cookie in her mouth. "What didn't he do?"

"Move here to be with me!"

Kaitlin almost choked on her cookie. "What?"

"Am I being greedy? I want love. I want companionship. I want happiness. And I want it now."

Her sister reached for her hand and squeezed. "It's gonna take time."

"I don't want it to." The chime from the grandfather clock in the next room caught her attention. "How'd you do it?"

"Do what?"

"How'd you manage the loneliness for all those years?"

Kaitlin was nibbling on another cookie. "That was different. Never had anyone, so I didn't know what I was missing."

Kelly nodded her head. "You have Jeremy now. What would you do if he suddenly left?"

Kaitlin put down her mug and wiped her hands on a napkin. She pushed her locks back behind her ears. "I don't know."

They stared at each other, silence between them. "Pray you never find out. 'Night, Katie." Kelly walked toward the stairs, slowly climbing them one by one, all alone.

***

Kelly finished her shift on Christmas Eve. She was walking to her car when Kaitlin texted, asking her to pick up a couple of quarts of eggnog for the next day. Kelly detoured to a convenience store. She was lost in thought as she approached the counter. Suddenly a voice brought her back to reality. That voice belonged to Todd.

"Hi, Kelly. Merry Christmas."

She turned to look at him. "Merry Christmas to you, too."

"Would it be all right if we talked for a moment?"

"What do you want?"

"I wanted to say I'm sorry one more time. You know, I may not have told you the complete truth, but I didn't really lie to you. I was engaged to Mandy and wanted to marry her, but when I met you, I couldn't help myself. It was like my eyes were suddenly opened. Everything became crystal clear. I fell in love with you."

Kelly noted his brown eyes were filled with sadness.

He looked down at the floor. "I can imagine how it seemed. I know I hurt you, but I'm still in love with you."

He reached for her, but she stepped backwards.

He frowned. "You can believe me or not, but I did decide to break it off with Mandy. I just didn't have a chance to do it before you came to the office."

A customer walked past, accidentally bumping into Todd, who checked his pockets, probably to make sure he still had his wallet, before turning to Kelly again.

"You're the one I want to share my life with, not her. I'd do anything for a second chance. This time, no secrets, just honesty. I won't continue to bother you, but if you feel anything, anything at all for me, please give me a second chance."

Kelly felt a sudden pang of longing, to hold him, to kiss him. Instead, she stared at him for a very long moment. "We'll see. Merry Christmas." She paid for the eggnog and left.

Driving home, she pondered their conversation. Did she still care for him? Was what he said true? If it had been true and if he'd broken it off, but told her afterwards, how would she have felt? Would she have stayed with him? And where exactly did Geeter fit in? She had been in love with Todd, but did she love Geeter? A horn from the car behind her brought her mind back to the present. Everyone was asleep when she finally arrived home early on Christmas morning. The questions in her mind delayed her sleep for hours.

***

The noise from downstairs woke Kelly. It was Christmas morning, exactly one year after Ballister left her. The pain suddenly cascaded down. She was helpless, lacking the strength to get out of bed. Tears seared her cheeks. She buried her head in her pillow. Kelly jumped when Kaitlin gently brushed her hair. Concern was showing on her sister's face. "Kel, what's wrong?"

Kelly sat up with her back to the headboard, drawing her knees to her chest. "You know what today is?"

Kaitlin's eyes were moist. "I know. I'm sorry. Hadn't seen you this morning. Came by to make sure you're okay."

Kelly sniffed her tears away as Kaitlin handed her a tissue. "This is unbearable. My life sucks."

"I wish I could make it better. Don't know what to say, other than I'll always be here for you."

Tears welled in Kelly's eyes again as they hugged. "You don't know how much that means."

Kaitlin dried her tears with her thumbs. "Wish there was more I could do for you."

Kelly stared off into space and didn't say anything.

Kaitlin's eyes became curious. "Penny for your thoughts?"

Kelly sniffed before replying, "You'd want change..."

"Try me, Kel, just try me."

Kelly was silent for a moment. "Okay, but remember, you asked for it. Guess who I ran into last night at the convenience store."

"I don't know, who?"

"Todd Andrews."

Kaitlin's eyes narrowed. "What did that scumbag want? I hope you didn't talk to him."

But Kelly had. She told Kaitlin everything he'd said. "I'm not sure, but I think I still have feelings for him."

Katie hissed, "After what he did to you? How could you?"

"You see, that's just it. Do I still love him, or is it just because I am so sick and tired of being alone? And then

112

there's Geeter. He's so nice and I really like him, but the distance... and how painfully slow it's going... makes me wonder what I should do. New York was magical, but it seems like it was decades ago."

Kaitlin sighed. "I'd never tell you what to do, but remember the old adage, 'Once a cheater, always a cheater.' Please be careful. I love you, and don't want to see you get hurt. I hate him for what he did. But no matter what, I'll support you, one hundred percent. I am and will always be in your corner."

Downstairs, the doorbell rang.

Kaitlin said, "You should probably get up soon. I expect everyone will start arriving shortly."

Kelly took a long hot shower, dressed, and descended the stairs. She did a double take when she saw who was sitting downstairs.

Chapter 24

Her ex-husband sat in the arm chair, playing with their children like nothing had happened. He'd brought presents and was all smiles as he watched the kids open them. Jeremy and Kaitlin sat protectively in the room along with her parents.

Jeremy looked like he wanted to take Ballister outside and kill him. Kelly wished he would. When her ex caught sight of her, he ran to her and wrapped her in an embrace. She didn't return the hug.

"Merry Christmas, Kelly. Wow! You look great!"

"What are you doing here?"

"It's Christmas. I wanted to see my children."

"You didn't want to see them last Christmas."

His expression was one of pain. "I was stupid. A midlife crisis. I can't make it up, but I want to come back into their lives."

Her entire body tensed. "That's a matter for the courts. You declared you never wanted to see them again and signed off all custodial and visitation rights. By law, you can't be here."

"I know. Saying I'm sorry will never make it right. You may not believe this, but I'm a changed man."

Kelly studied him through narrowed eyes. His physical appearance was different. His goatee and long hair were gone. His blond hair was flecked with gray, but the twinkle in his eyes was still strong.

Anger erupted. "What makes you think I would ever believe or trust you again?"

"There's nothing I can say, but in time my actions will show you I'm the same man you loved for all those years. I quit my job and moved here, just so I can be close to you and the kids." She started to protest, but he continued, "My hope is in time you'll forgive me. I went through a midlife crisis, Kelly. Looking back, I threw away everything I really wanted. I had it all, but squandered it. I'm sorry. Can you forgive me?"

Kelly walked toward him, smiling. He reached for her. Kelly raised her hand to slap him, but Kaitlin wrapped her arms around her from behind.

Ballister tried to push Kaitlin out of the way, but Jeremy grabbed him, forcibly dragging her ex into the next room.

***

Jeremy was breathing heavily as he stood in Ballister's way. "Time for you to leave. The kids can see you."

Ballister shoved Jeremy away from him, "Screw you! Who do you think you are? Patriarch of the family?"

A movement to his side caught Jeremy's attention. Stan—Kelly and Kaitlin's father—was at his side.

Despite his age, Stan shoved his finger in Ballister's face. "I'm the patriarch of this family. Get out of this house. You have three choices: A, leave on your own accord; B, I'll have Jeremy escort you off the property; or C, keep it up and the police will arrest you for trespassing. How do you want this to end?"

Jeremy placed his hand on Ballister's chest to keep him away from the old man.

"Screw you, Stan. I have a right to see my children, and today is Christmas. You can try to throw me out, but I'll be back tomorrow."

"Get a court order. After the way you hurt my daughter and grandchildren, I despise you. If I had the physical strength to do it, I'd kick your ass! Stay one minute longer and Jeremy will do it for me. Now leave!"

The children were still within listening distance. Little Davy cried as he ran into the room, clutching Jeremy's leg. He cried, "Daddy, scared!"

Jeremy picked him up. "Hush, Davy, it's okay. Just an adult thing. It's fine. Let Mimi hold you." Jeremy called for Nora. She took David and carried him into the other room.

When Jeremy turned back toward him, Ballister was seething. "Bastard! You make my son call you 'Daddy'? I always knew you were a jerk."

Jeremy's eyes narrowed, "He only calls me Daddy because the man who fathered him deserted him. Davy needed a father figure. You certainly weren't around. Now you show up like nothing happened? You're insane. Get out of here now!"

"Kiss my ass!"

Jeremy stepped toward him. "Leave this second before you do permanent psychological damage to your children. Want me to help you find the door?"

Before Ballister could reply, the doorbell rang. Stan opened it. Martina and her family were in the doorway. Jeremy could see they were stunned, seeing Ballister. Martina and her husband Gary were attorneys. Stan quickly brought them up to speed.

Martina stepped toward Ballister. "You have thirty seconds to remove yourself from this property, or I'm filing charges. I can assure you, I'll win this battle. Want to spend Christmas in jail?"

Kelly's ex shot them all the finger before he slammed the door behind him.

Jeremy's blood pressure was elevated. He started breathing slowly to calm himself.

Kaitlin screamed, "Jeremy! Get in here. Something's wrong with Kelly."

Jeremy beat everyone else into the next room. Kelly was on her knees, grasping at her chest.

Kaitlin's voice came out in clumps. "Said she was dizzy. Then she... she fell down. Says she has severe chest pain. What should we do?"

"Let's get her to the sofa and give her some space." Jeremy swept Kelly up in his arms and carried her to the couch.

Nora and Martina grabbed Kelly's children, shooing everyone out of the room.

Jeremy did a quick assessment and didn't like her color. Kelly's breathing was ragged. Jeremy's experience had mainly been with traumatic battle injuries, but he was getting scared. "Call an ambulance. Tell them Kelly may be having a heart attack."

Kelly tried to get up, protesting, "Don't call. I'm fine. Just need a few minutes."

The doorbell rang again and the door swung open. Kelly's other sister Cassandra and her family had arrived.

"What's going on?" Cassandra exclaimed. "I saw both Ballister and that doctor sitting in their cars outside." Kelly let out a sudden scream of pain. Cassandra barreled into the room. "Daddy, what's wrong with Kelly?"

Kaitlin and Jeremy exchanged a curious look. Jeremy said, "Hold up on the call to 911 for a second. Might get help quicker with Todd." Turning to Cassandra, he asked, "What was Andrews doing outside?"

"I don't know. Just sitting in his Beamer."

Jeremy again looked at Kaitlin. "If I'm not back in sixty seconds, make the call."

Jeremy grabbed his truck keys from his jacket. Running outside, he knew he couldn't head directly toward the silver BMW parked half a block away. Todd would take off. His truck was parked in by Kaitlin's Toyota. Firing it up, he backed as close to the garage door as he dared before cutting across the lawn. Jeremy cursed when the bumper of his four-wheel drive caught Kaitlin's Toyota in the headlight, peeling back the front quarter panel of her car.

As soon as he hit the street, Jeremy changed direction, flooring the accelerator. He covered the short distance rapidly as he headed toward the BMW.

The Beamer suddenly came to life as Todd smoked the tires, trying to get away. Jeremy could see him turn his wheel to the right to back into the neighbor's driveway to turn.

Before Todd could shift into forward, Jeremy blocked his escape with the truck, then jumped out and ran to the driver's side.

Todd's face was ashen.

Jeremy yelled through the closed window, "We need your help! Something's wrong with Kelly!"

"I don't believe you. I'm not opening the car door."

"I promise I won't hurt you. Kelly's having chest pain. Maybe a heart attack. Please help!"

Todd's mouth dropped open. He quickly opened the door. "Let me get my bag out of the trunk!"

The two of them ran toward the house. Inside, he knelt next to Kelly, listening to her heart with his stethoscope.

"Stop," Kelly said, pushing his hands away from her chest. "Keep your hands off me. There's nothing wrong with me that a little time won't take care of. I'm fine, really." She looked at Jeremy. "Please get him away from me."

Jeremy shook his head. "He's a doctor. He can help."

She glared at both of them.

Andrews pulled the stethoscope from his ears. "How are you feeling?"

"A little shaken up, that's all."

"Do you have any pain, anywhere?"

"My chest hurts a little, but I think it's anxiety."

"What's your pain level?"

"Maybe a six or seven."

He listened to her chest again. "Have you ever had a heart condition?"

"No, why?"

"Ever have heart palpitations?"

Jeremy exchanged a look of concern with Kaitlin. She walked over and grasped his hand. Kelly's voice rose. "Stop it. You're scaring me. What's going on?"

"Probably nothing, but you have arrhythmia. We need to get you to the hospital, stat." He turned to Kaitlin and said, "Call an ambulance. Tell them we have a thirty-three-year-old Caucasian female with moderate chest pain." He turned to Jeremy and added, "Quick! Get her an aspirin."

Kelly said, "I am not having a heart attack."

"We're not taking any chances. We'll get an EKG. Chances are it isn't a heart attack, but just in case..."

Jeremy was on the way back in when he heard Kelly ask, "Why were you outside?"

Todd blushed. "I was trying to get up the courage to knock on the door and wish you a Merry Christmas. Merry Christmas, by the way."

Kelly's face clouded. "I'm beginning to hate Christmas."

Jeremy handed Kelly the aspirin and a glass of water.

"It will be more effective if you chew it," Todd said.

"I know. I'm a nurse, in case you've forgotten."

"And I'm a doctor. You'll do what the doctor tells you."

"Who died and made you the boss?"

"Just do what I say. I'm going to have you admitted overnight for testing and—"

"We'll see what they say in the ER."

"Like hell. I asked you to chew that aspirin. Want me to crush it for you?"

Jeremy had enough of the banter. "I don't think this is helping the situation. Kelly, just chew the pill."

Kelly glared at Todd and did as instructed.

The paramedics arrived. Kelly refused to leave before she kissed her children, apologizing for ruining Christmas.

Nora reassured her in front of everyone, "It's okay, Mommy. That's what Mimi's are for, to help out when things like this happen. Don't worry about anything. I've got this."

"But Mom—"

"Don't forget I raised four girls and every one of them turned out perfect, just look at you."

Jeremy stifled a laugh as Nora winked at him.

Chapter 25

There was an emptiness in his soul. Life was miserable for Geeter ever since he'd said goodbye to Kelly in New York City. His heart pined for her so badly, he'd lost his appetite. Sarah told him it was because he was in love. Even though he and Kelly texted, talked daily, and Skyped a couple of times each week, life was unbearable.

Kelly was all he thought about. In his mind, he saw her everywhere. When he drove to town in the truck, if he turned his head quickly, she was there on the seat next to him. When he worked the fields, he would see her standing at the edge of the fence row. In his room at night, when he closed his eyes, her beautiful face was what he saw. Sarah was right. He was in love. He'd never felt like this in his entire life. But he hadn't confessed his true feelings to Kelly. He was afraid it would scare her away. Maybe he would tell her when they were face to face. When the time was right, he'd confess his love for her.

Geeter pulled up in front of Sarah's house and set the brake before turning off the ignition. Sarah was waiting on the porch. One of Burt's hounds sat on the steps, tail thumping loudly as he approached. Geeter scratched the dog's ears. Sarah was staring at the horizon.

"Merry Christmas, Sarah."

"You, too." She patted the glider next to her. "Come, sit a spell." Her hand was freezing when she grasped his. "They'd be proud of what you done with the farm."

"Wuddn't just me. It was us."

Sarah wiped her eyes. "I miss Mom so much. Daddy too, but Mom the most."

"I miss them, too."

They spent most of the morning sitting on the porch, reminiscing. Christmas had been his mother's favorite holiday. As they ate their Christmas meal in silence, all Geeter could think about was Kelly. They had planned to talk while she was driving to work in the afternoon. The tick-tock of the second hand on the grandfather clock sounded like something out of an Alfred Hitchcock movie, with enough time between the tocks to count to ten or twenty if you were really quick.

Geeter was not only counting down the seconds until he could talk to Kelly, but was counting down the minutes until he would leave on the thirtieth of December to visit. In his mind, he could already taste her lips, hear her beautiful voice, feel the warmth of her hands, and breathe in her delectable scent. Never before in his life had he been so in love. He couldn't wait to tell her in person.

After spending the morning with Sarah and Burt, he drove to the farm to feed the animals. The quacking duck alarm on his phone brought a smile to his face. It was time to call Kelly. Geeter speed dialed her number. His hands shook as he waited for her to answer. He cleared his throat and prepared to sing *White Christmas* because she said it was her favorite holiday song.

A voice answered, "Hey, Geeter." It wasn't Kelly.

"Jeremy? What the heck? I must have dialed wrong. I thought this was Kelly's phone."

Hesitation. "This is her phone."

Geeter's shoulders tensed. Ever since the day they'd met, Geeter had the feeling Jeremy wasn't keen about him dating Kelly. Maybe L.T. was going to tell him to quit calling. "Why'd you answer her phone then, L.T.? I do something wrong?"

"No. Something happened to Kelly."

Geeter's hands trembled as his voice rose an octave. "What happened? Please tell me she's all right. Was she in an accident?"

"No, nothing like that. She'll be just fine. Her ex-husband came over this morning and gave her a really hard time in front of the kids. When she started having chest pains, we took her to the hospital. Katie's with her. I'm on my way there now. Kelly gave me her phone because she knew you'd be calling. She didn't want for it to just ring and ring, not have anyone answer it, and you worry."

Geeter floored the accelerator. The dirt cloud chased after him as he raced down the back roads on the way to the farm. His next destination would be Chicago. "Worry? How can I not worry? Which hospital? I'm leaving right now."

"Whoa! Calm down! Katie said it was an anxiety attack, but there might be a problem with her heart. Nothing serious, but they're keeping her overnight for observation. You should wait before driving all the way up here. They're calling for some pretty nasty weather. Kelly will be well taken care of, if not spoiled, so you don't need to drop everything and come up here."

Geeter's breathing was labored. "L.T..."

Geeter heard Jeremy's voice, which seemed more understanding. "Look, I understand how it is when you really care for someone. The bottom line is, if you are coming, plan on staying with us."

Jeremy filled him in on the events of the morning in great detail.

Geeter power-braked to a stop in front of the farmhouse. "L.T., I'm gonna pay Ballister a nice little visit. When I get done with him—"

"Eighty-six that talk. You go through with that, you'll lose her for sure. She needs a man... not a hotheaded boy, understand?"

"Yes, sir."

"Geeter. We're friends. Don't call me 'sir' again. Got it?"

"Yes, sir."

"Drive carefully. Keep me updated."

Geeter packed his bags in record time. He finished feeding the animals before calling Sarah to take care of the farm for a couple of days.

By quarter of three, he had the cruise set to seventy-five miles an hour and was flying north on Interstate 65 toward Nashville. The trip was more than six hundred miles, but Geeter figured he could be there by early morning.

God, please take care of her.

As the miles sped by, he thought about his hopes and dreams. He hoped Kelly would fall in love with him. Geeter wanted to marry her, wishing she would move onto the farm with him. *Never believed I'd be lucky enough to have kids.* The thought of being a father to her children brought an overwhelming warmth to his chest. He and Kelly would make them so happy. He'd love them as his own. They'd love the farm. Celebrate holidays as a big family. He dreamed of kissing Kelly under the mistletoe, growing old with her at his side.

Geeter made it to Nashville in record time. But forty miles north of the Music City, freezing rain slowed him down. If he didn't heed the weather, he might wreck and delay his arrival.

Fear gnawed at his insides. Jeremy said it was nothing, but suppose Jeremy was wrong or hadn't told him everything? Maybe there was something seriously wrong with Kelly. For the first time in his life, Geeter knew exactly what he wanted. More than just wanted. He needed Kelly, more than anything else. But now he was scared for her wellbeing. He hadn't even been this scared when he got shot in Iraq.

The freezing rain turned to heavy snow. He remembered hearing the prediction for a dangerous winter storm to blanket the region. But his thoughts hadn't been on the snow, they were on Kelly. His worry increased with every passing mile. Never a praying man, he prayed now. *Please God, protect her, watch over her, take care of her. And if you need to take someone in her place, take me instead.*

Chapter 26

B efore noon the day after Christmas, Kelly stared at the blanket of snow from inside her hospital room.

Thirteen inches already covered Chicago and the weather man was calling for another eighteen before the storm moved on. The TV reporters were cautioning people to stay off the roads because the snow plows were having trouble keeping the major arteries open.

Kaitlin wheeled Kelly under the canopy where Jeremy was waiting with his truck. He lifted Kelly into the front seat before helping Kaitlin into the back. Normally, the trip would take about twenty minutes, but near white-out conditions made the drive considerably longer. They arrived home a little after two.

Pulling into the drive, Kelly asked, "Did Geeter get here yet?"

Kaitlin and Jeremy shared a worried glance.

Jeremy answered, "No, not yet. Talked to him early this morning. He was over halfway here, but the road conditions were pretty bad. I told him to hold up in a motel until the storm passed, but he refused. He forgot his phone charger and was almost out of juice. It's been about eight hours since I last spoke with him."

The heat from the defroster suddenly made it difficult to breathe. What was happening with Geeter? The tightness returned to her chest.

Events of the previous twenty-four hours left her mind fuzzy. First, her ex-husband's escapade brought this on. Then Todd had been sitting outside when her pain started. *Idiot.* His need to control her answered out loud, once and for all, whether she still had any feelings for him.

Then Jeremy arrived, telling her about Geeter's call. Kelly's heart warmed, like it had when they'd met. But with everything going on, she'd almost completely forgotten about Geeter. Obviously, he hadn't forgotten her, dropping everything, and risking his life to come be with her. The warmth stirring in her chest caught on fire.

Kaitlin had spent the entire Christmas evening by her side in the hospital. They'd talked about how even though she'd known him only a short time, Kelly realized how much she cared for Geeter. Kaitlin smiled knowingly, and then retold the love story she shared with Jeremy. As Kelly listened, she couldn't help wondering if it always took a problem to bring people together.

Kelly couldn't wait to see her children. She jumped down from the truck, but slipped in the snow. Jeremy was quick enough to catch her. Lifting Kelly in his arms, he waited until Kaitlin linked her arm through his. Together, they worked their way into the house.

Kelly's family was waiting at the door, and smothered her with hugs, but the sweetest ones were from her children. The homey smell of roasted turkey filled the air. Apparently the family had waited until she arrived to eat, celebrating with thanks her return. Although it had been hard to make the children wait, some of the children's Christmas gifts had been saved so Kelly could watch them open them. Then, the entire family sprawled in the family room to watch movies together.

Thank you, Lord, for my family. Kelly also said a prayer asking God to watch out for Geeter. He had left

Chattanooga over twenty-four hours earlier. Her chest tightened as fear crept into her mind.

During the third movie of the afternoon, Jeremy's phone rang. Kelly's interest piqued when he excused himself.

Jeremy returned, looking worried. Kelly was on her feet. "Was that Geeter?"

"Yes. His truck slid into a ditch. Walked three miles in the snow until he found a house. I'm going to get him. Be back soon."

Kaitlin stood. "I'll go with you."

Jeremy shook his head. "No, honey, the roads are bad. Suppose I get stuck?"

"Then I'll be there with you." He started to protest, but Kaitlin stomped her foot. "This is not open for discussion. I almost lost you twice. I won't risk it again. Either we go together, or you don't go at all."

***

Kelly had tucked her children in, and her parents had gone to bed. Her brother-in-law John had run the snow blower before turning in. Kelly aimlessly flipped through the channels while she waited. Lights flashed through the picture window—lights from Jeremy's truck. Despite being told to take it easy and rest, Kelly jumped up to throw open the door.

Her heart was pounding as Geeter emerged from the rear door, waving. He ran through the snow, taking the porch steps two at a time. He wrapped his arms tenderly around her. The taste of his lips took her back to New York City.

Jeremy carried Kaitlin in his arms but had to wait for Geeter and Kelly to pause.

When they passed, Kaitlin whispered to Kelly, "Merry Christmas, Kel."

Chapter 27

G eeter crawled across the soft carpet as he chased Davy. The baby laughed with joy. Melinda and Tessa ambushed him, jumping on his back. He rolled, tickling the girls' ribs as they screamed with glee. K.J. came to their rescue, hopping onto Geeter's belly to tickle him.

The days between Christmas and New Year's Eve had gone exceptionally fast, but were the happiest of his life. The warm hospitality of the Jenkins family and bonding with Kelly's brood brought out feelings he never expected. Her children accepted him and loved playing with him. He didn't have a lot of time with Kelly, but what they did share was wonderful.

Kelly seemed to be perpetually exhausted, though Geeter made sure to help, taking some of the burden from her. Kelly smiled as Geeter played with the kids, getting down to their level. Sometimes Jeremy would join in and the two men would engage the children for hours. Both of them were very good at imitating voices, and the stories they came up with filled the children with raucous laughter.

On the morning of New Year's Eve, Kelly was enjoying time with her mom and three sisters upstairs. Stan had taken Kelly's brothers-in-law, with the exception of Jeremy to an indoor driving range. Geeter and Jeremy had all the kids down in the family room, carrying on and having a ball. Geeter tried to keep the kids' outrageous laughter down to a roar, but failed miserably.

***

At half past ten, Kelly heard the doorbell ring.

Jeremy yelled from the family room, "I'll get it!"

Kelly and the girls kept talking, that is until Jeremy walked in. The children must have been playing makeup because numerous hair ties decorated his short hair.

Everyone laughed, but Kaitlin immediately quieted. "What's wrong?"

Jeremy looked embarrassed as he handed an envelope to Kelly. "Kelly, I'm sorry. That was a deputy from the sheriff's office. It's a summons for you to appear in family court next week."

Kelly read the document. The nagging pain started again. She grasped her chest. Her ex-husband had filed papers to obtain visitation rights and partial custody of their children.

Kaitlin was immediately by her side, comforting her.

Martina grabbed the summons and read it out loud. She turned to Kelly. "Don't worry. Our best attorneys will be there for you. He won't get custody. You have my word on that!"

Kelly's chest tightened further. *This is so unfair.* How could Ballister suddenly reappear and wreak havoc on her world? Cassandra joined Kaitlin in comforting her sister.

Martina paced the room, her anger plain for all to see. "How dare he think he can just walk away from you? No, *abandon* you, then just walk back into your life and take control like nothing ever happened? Ballister better think again. He messed with the wrong family."

***

Geeter and Cassandra's oldest daughter Ellie were leading the children in a game of follow the leader. The sound of footfalls on the wooden stairs caught his attention. Jeremy motioned Geeter aside, telling him about the summons. Geeter slowly ascended the steps. He stood at the top, waiting until Kelly saw him. It seemed to take forever for her eyes to notice him. She reached for him. Geeter held her against him, and softly stroked her soft hair as he comforted her.

She pulled him toward the kitchen.

"What can I do to help?"

She turned, her warm hand clinging to his. "Nothing. This is my issue, not yours. I have to deal with that... that... that idiot, somehow."

Geeter gently cupped her face so their eyes could meet. "You're wrong, Kelly. Your fight's my fight. Your pain's my pain. If you don't want my help, I understand. But if you do, I'm here. I'll always be here. Want me to talk to him?"

Kelly shook her head. "No, please don't. He's playing mind games with me. I never told anyone this, not even Katie, but he did this all the time. Sometimes, he was so cruel."

She pulled away to grab a tissue. "It's strange. I used to feel so blessed and happy, but I was only being played for a fool." She buried her head in her hands. Geeter held her in his arms.

It didn't bother Geeter when people hurt him, but now that Kelly was the one hurting, it was different. *If Ballister was here, I would...* The gall the man had. Turning his back on his own children was unbelievable. But to hurt Kelly was criminal.

When the men returned, Martina filled them in and called for a family council. The adults gathered in the kitchen. Geeter retreated downstairs with the children, but less than five minutes later, Jeremy called his name.

"Geeter, come up to the meeting."

Geeter looked away. "Not part of the family, L.T."

"Yeah, you are. Kelly sent me to get you."

Geeter didn't move.

Jeremy's voice changed to that of a drill sergeant. "This is a direct order from your former superior officer. Get your butt moving, or I'll drag you upstairs!"

Geeter stood, then slowly walked upstairs, the angry voices that sometimes haunted him nibbling at the corner of his mind. Geeter willed them away.

In the kitchen, Martina was directing the conversation, outlining their strategy. Geeter stood outside the ring of the family.

Martina's husband Gary was also a lawyer. He said, "We'll ask the judge to throw out Ballister's request, disclosing the sudden abandonment of his wife and children. The only concern will be which judge gets assigned to the case."

Martina replied, "I have no experience in Family Court. The summons said the judge is Julie Patterson. Do you know her?"

Gary frowned. "Yes, I do. Very conservative. She'll be protective of the children's rights, but she'll also be favorable to the father's requests. Even so, she isn't likely to grant him joint custody until he has shown merit. Unfortunately, she'll likely grant visitation. We need a strategy if she does." He turned to Kelly. "If it goes that way, we should petition for supervised visits. When it's convenient for you. You willing to be there when he visits with the children?"

Wrinkles appeared around Kelly's eyes, as if she were aging in front of Geeter. She winced. "I can't do that."

Gary nodded. "In that case, the judge will give you two options. Using a court-appointed custodian or allowing you to have someone else, someone whom you trust be there. Martina and I would volunteer, but the judge will turn that down since we're representing you."

Kelly replied, "I want Jeremy and Kaitlin to supervise the visits." She turned to them. "If that's okay with you."

Kaitlin touched Kelly's shoulder. "Absolutely. We're there for you and your children, always."

Jeremy added, "Family's always first. Our answer's a resounding yes."

The meeting wound down. Kelly withdrew into an invisible shell. Over the following days, Geeter tried to cheer her up, but she totally ignored him. *Seems like I no longer exist.* Maybe it was time to go home.

Chapter 28

T he courtroom smelled like lemon furniture polish. Kelly sat in the front row, Kaitlin and Nora holding her hands. Behind her sat the men.

Ballister strutted in with his attorney. Gary had provided Kelly with the best domestic issue attorney on his staff, Leslie Anton. Just before the judge walked in, Leslie motioned for Kelly to sit next to her. All eyes were on her, boring into her soul, or so it seemed.

The judge entered the courtroom. The bailiff called the court to order, "All rise for the honorable Judge Patterson."

Patterson adjusted herself in her seat. "You may be seated. First case?"

Ballister's attorney started out by reviewing the petition, asking the judge to grant joint custody and unlimited visitation rights to his client. Kelly looked fearfully at her attorney, but Leslie patted her hand. "It'll be fine."

Judge Patterson asked Kelly's ex to come to the stand.

His voice sounded sincere. "Your honor, I made a monumental mistake last year. I became infatuated with one of my patients and allowed her to talk me into leaving my wife and children for her. I was flattered, and that flattery led to mental confusion. The woman led me astray, divorcing me shortly after she married me. I was temporarily insane."

Judge Patterson asked a few more questions before calling Kelly to the stand, asking for her side of the story.

"Your honor, we were in Hawaii for my sister's wedding. It was Christmas Day, and he received a call. I asked who it was, but his answer was vague. When we had our family get together, he claimed he was sick and didn't come. But when I returned, he was already packed. He told me he was divorcing me. I asked if we could talk it out, and he said no. He wanted a divorce. He left without even saying goodbye to his children."

The judge asked a few more questions before retiring to her chamber. She returned and, just as Gary had predicted, denied joint custody. She told Ballister that he must first prove himself. She did grant him four hours of visitation rights each week.

Attorney Anton asked the judge if those visits could be supervised. Ballister's attorney asked for a reason. Anton replied, "Your client is pleading temporary insanity. By his own admission, he exhibited unusual behavior. I don't believe the court should allow any child to be in the unsupervised presence of someone who admitted even the remote possibility of insanity."

The judge replied, "Is Ms. Jenkins able to supervise these visits?"

"No, your honor. Ms. Jenkins requests Mr. and Mrs. Jeremy Roberts to act in her stead."

Patterson turned to Ballister's attorney. "Is your client in agreement, counselor?"

Before his attorney could answer, Ballister jumped up. "I object very much! Do you know that man..." he pointed at Jeremy, "...makes my children call him 'Daddy'? And I would have to have him in the room while I see the children I fathered? How fair is that, I ask you?"

The judge slammed her gavel down. "Another outburst like that, and I will have you removed from this courtroom, Mr. Ballister!" Turning to Anton, she asked, "Is this true?"

"No, your honor. But Mr. Roberts has been the sole constant male in the children's life. The children haven't seen Mr. Ballister in over a year."

Ballister jumped to his feet again. "That's because he has what's rightfully mine. My wife lives with him. My children are controlled by him! He took away everything I had. Can't you see this, judge?"

Judge Patterson slammed her gavel, instructing the bailiff to remove Ballister from the courtroom. After the bailiff returned, Patterson addressed Kelly. "Are any of your ex-husband's accusations founded?"

Kelly's chest tightened. The air thickened, refusing to enter her lungs. The room started spinning. "No, your honor!"

"But your address and Mr. Roberts' address *are* the same, aren't they?"

"Yes. We live with Jeremy, I mean Mr. Roberts, and Kaitlin. His wife lives there, too. It's not like he and I are living together!"

"I see. What about controlling your children? What are his interactions with them?"

"Well, both he and my sister take care of them when I can't. Actually, he helps out quite a bit."

"In what way?"

Kelly was starting to sweat. "I don't know! He, uh, bathes them, feeds them, reads stories with them, plays with them, nurtures them."

"In other words, he does all the things a father would do for his children, correct?"

"Yes, but Kaitlin, my sister, also does the same!"

"But she's not a man, is she?"

"Katie? Of course not!"

139

"So, despite your husband or rather ex-husband's outburst and flaws, he did say some words of truth, didn't he?"

Kelly began to panic. The axis of the spinning room shifted. Jeremy and Kaitlin's faces were red with anger.

The judge cleared her throat. "I am inclined to agree with Mr. Ballister that having visitation supervised by Mr. Roberts is not a viable option. The court will appoint a custodian to supervise the visits. The visits will be between 10 A.M. and 2 P.M. every Saturday." She studied Kelly. "We will meet in three months to determine the effects of visitation and consider custody."

The room spun faster, growing dark as the floor rushed upward.

***

The strong taste of morning coffee didn't even help his despair. Geeter read the writing on the wall. After the court date, Kelly grew silent. She only responded to her children, mother and sister, Kaitlin. She ignored everyone, including Jeremy and Geeter. He had to get through to her.

Geeter waited until he could speak with her, when just the two of them were together. "What can I do to help you?"

The hopefulness evaporated when her vacant eyes met his.

"There is nothing you can do. I told you that earlier."

"But I think if you let me in, I could help. I came up here to make your life easier."

Kelly touched his cheek. "You're sweet. But this is like going through hell. You couldn't possibly understand or help."

"Try me, Kelly."

"I know you're trying to be nice, but this is something I have to do by myself." Kelly hung her head and walked away from him.

The next morning, Geeter shoved his duffel bag into his truck. The faces of Kelly's children were pressed against the living room window, watching him. The bond he felt to them was undeniable. *Gotta be strong for them.* When he walked back inside, the children hugged his knees, begging, "Please don't go!"

Geeter dropped to the floor to wrap them in a hug. They squiggled in his arms, smelling like summer sunshine. He forced happiness into his voice. "It's only for a little while! Maybe Momma will bring y'all down to my farm."

A tingle crawled up his spine. Eyes were on him. He looked up and found Kelly standing there, her heavy sweater wrapped around her shoulders as she stared at him.

Her voice was soft, but strong. "Kids, give Mommy a few minutes, okay?" She waited until they left. She made no move toward him. "I take it you're leaving now?"

He stared at his shoes. "Yeah. Gotta get home. Lots to do before spring plantin' time."

The distance between them was like a deep chasm. Her eyes were fixed on his. "Sorry I didn't spend more time with you."

"I understand. A lot going on. It's okay."

She shook her head. "No, it's not. You made a special trip up here to support me and I basically ignored you. I don't know what you think of me right now." She sniffled.

Geeter brushed the toe of his shoe over a spot on the carpet. "I think the world of you." He raised his eyes to see her face. "I care for you very much." The words he had planned to tell her were on his lips. But her eyes didn't meet his. The time to reveal his innermost thoughts had passed. "It's best if I leave. You and the kids ever want to come down, you're always welcome."

Kelly's eyes finally met his. "Geeter, it's not like... I just feel..."

"Feel what, Kelly? Please tell me. What do you really feel?"

"I... I... I don't know what I feel. You're one of the truest friends I ever had, but I don't know if..." Her voice trailed off.

His world was ending. Kelly was dumping him. The angry demon voices in his mind screamed at him. It took all of his resolve not to show his emotions. He'd hoped Kelly would tell him she loved him as much as he loved her. But she didn't. He needed to leave before he lost it in front of her. "I understand. Take care and call if you need me. Bye, Kelly." He stuck out his hand.

"Does this mean we aren't going to talk or text every day? I need you, Geeter!" Her eyes widened. For the first time, he noticed how bloodshot they were.

"You can call or text whenever you need to and I'll be there for you."

When she didn't move toward him, he took her hand and squeezed it. The kids were in the doorway to the next room, watching. Breathing deeply, he walked to them. Kneeling, he hugged each of her children before looking at her one last time. Her cheeks were moist as she stood like a statue. *Can't take this. Gotta go, now.* He tipped his hat, and started walking to his truck and, he guessed, out of her life.

Chapter 29

K elly hated Saturdays. The supervised visits were very tense. Ballister tried to drag them out, pushing the envelope by wanting to take his children "out." Removing the children from the home had been forbidden by the court order. Ballister was too strong willed for the original court-appointed custodian, so the court replaced her with a much sterner one. This man had been a desk sergeant for the Chicago Police Department. He took no grief from anyone and especially seemed to dislike Ballister.

On the last Saturday in January, Jeremy made a special breakfast of scrambled eggs, biscuits, and sausage gravy. He was putting it on the table when the cheesy smell of the omelet hit Kelly. Her morning coffee rushed to get out of her body. She ran toward the bathroom, only to find Kaitlin already clutching the rim of the toilet. Kelly had to use the sink.

Footsteps echoed behind her. Jeremy had followed.

"Katie, are you okay?"

Kaitlin wiped her mouth, but before she could answer, she wretched again.

Jeremy held his wife's long hair out of the way. He stared at Kelly. "Was it the eggs or the gravy?"

"No, Jeremy, I think..." She didn't finish because her stomach emptied itself again.

Kaitlin caught her breath. "Jeremy, please give us a few minutes, okay?"

***

Kaitlin stumbled back to the dining room. Everyone else was eating breakfast. Jeremy looked puzzled, and asked his mother-in-law, "Should we be eating this food? The smell made both of them sick."

Nora and her husband Stan exchanged a funny look as they smiled at each other. "Jeremy, I don't know what's wrong with Kelly, but I'm pretty sure Katie's sickness has nothing to do with the food."

Jeremy stared at Kaitlin. "Then what is it?"

Kaitlin's smile was so wide. She stood up, and walked over to kiss her husband's forehead. She whispered into his ear, "Congrats, Daddy!"

Kaitlin's hands trembled. Her vision blurred with happiness.

Jeremy danced around the room. "I'm gonna be a daddy. I love you, Katie."

"Love you, too, Daddy."

***

Kelly stared at her reflection in the mirror. The woman staring back at her was someone she no longer knew.

After breakfast, Jeremy drove to the drug store, and returned with a box of early pregnancy tests. Kaitlin's result was positive. The pair celebrated.

Kelly excused herself. In the bathroom, the test box was sitting on the rear of the commode. The wrapper crinkled as she removed the remaining test.

Afterward, she read the results. *God, no!* For Kaitlin and Jeremy, who had been trying to conceive for six months, the occasion was joyous. But Kelly's results deepened her depression.

When the crusty old custodian knocked on the door for Ballister's visit, she left for a walk. She needed somebody to talk to. She desperately wanted to talk to Geeter and be comforted by his voice. But since his departure three weeks earlier, he had been elusive, ignoring her calls. His farm work kept him busy, but he also seemed to be distancing himself from her. She couldn't blame him.

Kelly couldn't talk with Kaitlin and ruin her sister's happiness. There were no close friends at work she trusted to talk to. As far as her friends from L.A., well none of them had ever been true friends. She thought briefly about calling her two older sisters, but Martina would lecture her. Cassandra would chastise her. Talking with them was out of the question.

Snowflakes caught in her bangs as Kelly suffered alone. She muttered, "How will I feed a fifth child?" How could this have happened? Why did this happen to her? "I don't even know who the father is." She had used protection with both Todd and Geeter. Of course condoms weren't completely effective, but couldn't God give her a break?

The coldness of the day mirrored the weather in her mind. When a man's voice softly called her name, she was shocked to find her legs already snow covered. It was nearly dark.

"Kelly, you all right?"

She turned. Jeremy was standing there, concern obvious in his eyes. She quickly wiped her cheeks, and started to stand. Jeremy's eyes searched her face. "It'll be all right, you'll see. You aren't alone."

She choked back tears. "What are you doing here, Jeremy? You should be home with Katie."

"She's a little nauseous and wanted to take a nap. Everyone noticed you were missing. Katie was concerned and asked me to find you."

Kelly made a line in the snow with her shoe. "I'm fine. Just needed a little me-time, but I'm fine, perfectly fine."

"Liar," he said in a matter-of-fact manner.

Something snapped within her. Anger boiled from every pore, filling her heart and mind until it spilled from her lips. She shoved him. "What's that supposed to mean, jerk?"

His look of shock slowly faded. "The EPT box had two tests. Katie used one. The box is empty now. You took a pregnancy test today, too. It was positive, wasn't it?"

Kelly backed away. In the last year, Jeremy had become closer than a brother to her. After Kaitlin, he was her next best friend. In many respects, he treated her better than Ballister ever had. He treated her children as if they were his own. He bathed them, fed them, and tucked them in at night. He packed her lunches for work. He made sure her car always had gas and was maintained to perfection.

The nearby lamp post flickered to life. What Jeremy had done in the past didn't matter right now. Him being here, invading her solitude, irritated her beyond belief. She was pissed. She was hurt. Someone needed to pay. If Jeremy wanted to invade her world, he deserved it.

She hissed, "It's none of your damned business."

While he didn't verbally respond, his face reddened. He looked down, avoiding eye contact. "Sorry, Kelly. Didn't mean to offend you. I just care about you, that's all. Would you like me to walk you home?"

Her face was on fire. Jeremy was acting as if he was so much better than her. She unloaded on him. "You care for me, Jeremy? How much?" She grabbed his collar, pulling his lips close enough to hers that she could feel his breath. "Care enough to leave Katie for me? Enough to make my life a fairy tale?"

He recoiled, pushing her away. He looked confused.

"Didn't think so. Don't you ever tell me how much you care for me, understand? And while we're at it. Why are you always sticking your nose in my business? You're not my husband or lover or real brother or anything to me."

The loss of color in his face was evident, even in the dimming light.

Kelly didn't care. "In fact, what are you even doing here? Since I came here, you've acted like you own me or something. You are even more controlling than Todd was at the hospital!" Kelly's anger was building like flood water against a levy. She welcomed the warmth of her emotion. "You act like my children are yours, even to the point where David thinks you're his daddy. You treat my girls like they're your daughters. You play ball with K.J. almost every night, and I know he loves you more than me. You're just a constant reminder I don't have a husband."

Fugitive drops of saliva dripped from her lips. She wiped her face with her sleeve. But the buildup of bitterness continued to spew from her mouth.

"And look at the way you and Katie hang on each other, like a pair of adolescents in heat... you only do that to show me how 'great' you are, to remind me I don't have someone in my life. You can go to hell!"

Jeremy remained emotionless. "I'm truly sorry, Kelly. I'll take your response as a 'no' and see you at the house." He turned to swiftly walk away.

Kelly sat on the bench, fuming. But as she sat there, she replayed every word she'd muttered. The cold air slowly drained her wrath. Her heart ached, and she regretted what she had said. *What's wrong with me?*

Was she doomed to drive away everyone who cared about her?

Chapter 30

T he reassuring glow of the fireplace welcomed her. Was it all in her mind, or did everyone treat her differently? Her children were playing with their grandparents and didn't even look up. Jeremy steered clear of her and avoided eye contact. Kaitlin looked wistfully at her but didn't speak a word. Kelly was in her own little lonely world. The family seemed to sense she needed her space and that was exactly what she got for the entire week.

During the weekly visitation the following Saturday, Kaitlin took her out to a late lunch to get her away from the house. They were almost finished eating when Kaitlin asked, "Is something bothering you?"

Kelly shrugged her shoulders. "Nope."

"Liar! You might be able to convince others, but I know you too well!"

Kelly's rage went from zero to sixty. "Why do you think you can call me a liar? I know. Miss Perfect thinks she's better than me because she has a father for her baby and I don't. What gives you the right? If you didn't have Jeremy, you wouldn't act so high and mighty!" Kelly's voice was so loud, people at the adjacent tables were beginning to stare.

The outburst brought tears to Kaitlin's eyes. She nodded. "Jeremy was right."

"Right about what?"

"Oh, actually, many things. He told me he was pretty sure you were pregnant. He told me that calling you a liar was the hot button to push if I wanted to set you off. He told me to ignore the hatred and anger that would come out of you. He said it isn't really you or what you truly feel, but instead it's a combination of your circumstances and runaway hormones. He also said you needed professional help."

Kelly's mouth dropped open, but her little sister smiled sweetly and sipped on her coffee.

Suddenly Kaitlin's smile disappeared as a look of seriousness took over. She pointed a finger at Kelly's face. "I love you, Kelly, and I know it was the emotions. Whatever you said to him, he won't tell me, other than you were mean, but if you ever treat Jeremy like you did last Saturday, there'll be hell to pay."

Kelly was taken aback. "What's that supposed to mean?"

Kaitlin didn't back off. "It means you shouldn't take your frustrations out on the one man who's bent over backwards to help you and your kids."

Kelly's eyes narrowed. "I get it! He put a ring on your finger and that means more to you than the blood we share!" The volume of Kelly's voice eclipsed the noise of the restaurant. Everyone in the restaurant stared at them, but Kelly didn't care.

She wanted a fight. Her fingers trembled from inactivity.

"What? Nothing to say, you little bitch?"

Kaitlin studied her sister. "You want a fight? I won't give you one." She reached across the table to touch Kelly's hand. "You're under a lot of stress, but it'll be okay. We're here for you. We both love and care about you. You don't have to go through this alone." Kaitlin smiled. "Just consider how fortunate we are to be pregnant at the same time. We can shop for the babies together."

Kaitlin always saw the good in everything. *Because Mom and Dad gave you everything.* She was the baby of the family. Their parents had made it plain to see they loved precious little Kaitlin the most. *Bitchy little spoiled prima donna.*

Kelly slapped Kaitlin's hand away. "You really are a silly, naïve, stupid little baby, aren't you?" She was almost screaming. "All you can think about is your damn child when I don't even know if I want to have another baby. Maybe I'll get an abortion!"

Kaitlin's face contorted. "Kelly, no, don't say that! If you don't want the baby, let Jeremy and me adopt it. We'll care for your child as our own!"

Want it all, don't you? "Doesn't that just beat all? You get everything, huh? Your kid and mine, all for you and Mr. Caring Jeremy! If you just knew, Kaitlin, if you only knew how much he really cared. Of course, being such a simple, stupid girl, you don't realize the bond our children have in common."

Kaitlin's expression filled with confusion. "What?"

"Their father!"

Kaitlin's eyes grew wide. "What? What are you saying?"

Kelly drew satisfaction from the pain now obvious in Kaitlin's face. Kelly had suffered for so long. It was time to share the wealth. She smiled at her sister. "Your husband's good at not only saying it, but showing how much he cares." She waited until the fear on Kaitlin's face caught up to her inference. "He proved it, over and over again until we were both satisfied! So when you see him, ask your Prince Charming who the father of my child is."

Kaitlin stumbled and grabbed for a chair to keep her from falling. Kaitlin's limbs trembled violently. Her breathing became labored. "You slept with my husband? How could you?"

Kelly laughed. "That's right! And your husband told me I was so much better in bed than you ever were and that he loved me more than he ever loved you. At least I'm not a simple, stupid, childish bitch like you who is too stupid to realize what's going on!"

Tears ran down her sister's face, but they could have been kerosene for the way they fueled Kelly's anger.

"Now that you know the truth, I'm moving out to get away from you and that worthless husband of yours!" Kelly stood, slapped a twenty-dollar bill on the table, and stormed out.

***

Kaitlin grasped the table to keep from falling. Every eye was on her, but she couldn't help it. The air was suddenly stifling. Ever since she had met Jeremy, she feared he'd leave her for someone better. What Kelly had told her couldn't be true, could it?

Nagging accusations tortured her mind. He always seemed to be touching Kelly. Look how quickly he reacted to carry her into the house. They constantly shared private little jokes and laughs... *Oh my God!* If he ever wanted to... Kaitlin put her hand over her mouth to prevent throwing up. In her mind, Kelly was prettier, shapelier, her voice sweeter, her smile wider. Kaitlin couldn't compete. The room was spinning.

She used the tablecloth to catch the food that wouldn't stay down. Jeremy loved her, didn't he? *Did he really sleep with my sister?* As she fought back tears, her heart screamed not to believe it. She had seen his eyes. Down inside, she knew Jeremy loved only her. Even if he did want Kelly, he wouldn't give in, would he? She needed to know for sure, needed to talk to him, see the look on his face in person when she confronted him. She paid the rest of the bill and walked outside to discover Kelly had driven off, leaving her stranded at the restaurant.

***

The smell of baby powder filled the air. Jeremy was changing David when his cell rang. He placed it on speaker. "Hey, gorgeous! How is the world's most beautiful woman?"

It was Kaitlin, but she sounded as if she'd been crying. "Knock it off! Kelly stranded me at the restaurant. Pick me up, now."

"What happened?"

"Just get down here, now!" She disconnected.

Jeremy shivered. Kaitlin hadn't spoken to him like that since those first miserable days on the road when she'd been his boss. Jeremy found Nora downstairs and whispered, "Kelly and Kaitlin must've had a bad fight. I'm going to pick Katie up."

As he walked past the living room, he noted Ballister playing with K.J. K.J. seemed to be the only one of his children Ballister cared about. His twin daughters were staring at the man who used to be their loving father, the man who now ignored them. The custodian glanced at Jeremy but returned his gaze to Ballister. As always, Ballister ignored everyone but K.J.

Jeremy made record time getting to the restaurant. He shoved the truck into park. He started to get out to open the door for Kaitlin, but she climbed in. "Park this thing. We're gonna talk. Now, Roberts!"

Please let the baby be all right. He'd never seen her this angry. What had happened between Katie and Kelly? Everything in the world could be going to hell, but it'd be fine as long as he and Katie were on the same page. But they weren't on the same page or even in the same book... or maybe even in the same library. He found an open spot and parked, then turned to her. "What happened? Tell me what's wrong."

"Do you still love me, Jeremy? Am I still attractive? Am I still the girl of your dreams?"

"Yes. You're everything to me. I love you."

Tears were dribbling from her eyes. Her breathing was uneven. Jeremy reached out to hold her hand. Kaitlin pulled away. "Don't touch me."

"I don't understand. What's happening?"

Her face grew pale. The look in her eyes brought back a very unpleasant memory. He had seen the same hopelessness and despair in the mirror when he lost his parents. "When did you stop loving me?"

"What?"

"Do you think I'm ugly?"

"Katie, no. I think you're beautiful."

"Really? Is Kelly prettier than me?"

"No. You're the most beautiful..."

Her eyes clenched tight as she covered her ears. "Stop it, stop it, stop it!"

Jeremy grasped her hands. She pushed him away again. "Katie?"

"Who's the father of Kelly's child?"

What? Where did that come from? "I guess either Todd or Geeter. Why ask me?"

The color of her face was like something he had never seen. Most of her face was snow white, but dark blotches stained her cheeks. Jeremy worried about her health.

Kaitlin's gaze concentrated on his eyes. "Jeremy, I trusted you with my heart, my soul. Be honest with me. Our future depends on it."

Whatever was happening was well out of Jeremy's reasoning. He dug in his pocket for his phone. He considered calling for an ambulance. "I'm always honest with you."

She leaned hard against the seat. Kaitlin shook her head as she watched him.

Jeremy reached for her. Once again, she recoiled from his touch.

Kaitlin drew a deep breath. "Is she, is she... is Kelly carrying your child?"

What in the world? His eyes narrowed. "How could you even think that?" Her right eye twitched repeatedly. She looked away from him. *I think I understand.* He reached for and found her hands. She tried to push him away, but he held them tightly. "Did Kelly tell you I'm the father?"

Her gaze was focused in the distance. Almost absentmindedly, she nodded ever so slightly. "She told me you slept with her. And... and she told me you said she wasn't only better in bed than me but that you, you... loved her more than you ever loved me!"

"Katie..."

"I understand." Her moist eyes sought his. "She's beautiful and sweet. I can understand why you would want to sleep—"

Jeremy pulled Kaitlin in his arms. "Now you listen here. I love you, only you. I have since the day we met. I would never, could never do that." He pulled back, grasping her arms tightly in his hands. His face was almost nose to nose against hers. "I love you, Katie. I didn't even so much as flirt with her. Kelly lied to you."

After all they did to help her, Kelly had betrayed them. Her lies had hurt his wife. He finally understood Kelly's end game. She knew Kaitlin's deepest, darkest fears and viciously played on them. And Kaitlin had believed her. Jeremy's love hadn't been enough.

Kaitlin wrapped her arms around him. "I'm sorry. I knew it couldn't be true."

Jeremy sighed. "I'm the one who's sorry."

She pulled back to study his face. "Sorry for what?"

"Obviously I didn't make you feel loved enough. You doubted me. You thought I cheated on you."

"Baby, I'm sorry. She's my sister, my closest friend, besides you. I was so confused inside. I'm sorry I doubted you."

"It's okay. Don't worry about it."

"You don't understand. It wasn't really you I doubted. It was me."

His eyebrows raised in confusion. "You? You doubted yourself? What do you mean?"

She gripped his hands tightly enough to make his fingertips tingle. "I'm a plain, ordinary girl, nothing special at all. And I don't deserve the love you give me."

He cupped her chin, slowly kissing her nose. "Kaitlin Elizabeth Roberts, you're the queen of my life. I love you, forever. I'm the one who isn't worthy enough..."

He didn't have the opportunity to finish. Kaitlin wrapped her arms around his neck and buried her lips against his.

***

Kelly was waiting for them in the living room. *What is wrong with me?* Kelly needed to make this right.

It was after 10:00 P.M. when Jeremy and Kaitlin walked through the front door. Kelly reached for Kaitlin's hand, but her sister walked around her on her way up the stairs.

"I need to apologize to both of you. I-I-I don't know what got into me. I lied, Katie. Jeremy never slept with me. I apologize, Jeremy, for that lie. He never touched me or even kissed me. I'm sorry. Please forgive me. I don't understand what happened. Can we talk this out and get past it?"

Kaitlin's expression was blank. She turned to her sister. "Oh. So it's fine for you to lie to me, to make me believe my husband slept with you. And then you want to act like nothing happened?"

"I was just so angry and..."

"And you treated your sister like a punching bag," Jeremy said harshly. "Your life is screwed up, so why not screw hers up, too?"

Kaitlin grabbed Kelly's face and turned it toward her. "And to think I idolized you when I was young. I wanted to be like you. Boy, was I a fool."

Kelly reached up and locked on Kaitlin's forearms.

"Get your filthy hands off me, Kelly. I held back earlier, but I won't make that mistake again."

Kelly's chest pounded and grew tighter by the second. "Katie, wait, let me explain..."

Jeremy pinched both her wrists in a way that made her release Kaitlin's arms. "Both of you, please listen to me."

"What, are you going to tell Katie? Another lie? Maybe that I fathered all your kids?"

"No! I don't know what happened. I got so angry, so mad. I was jealous of you and wanted you to hurt like I did."

"You deserve a gold star for that one, sis. Now, get out of my way."

"Wait. I want to make this right. We live in the same house and I..."

Jeremy interrupted. "Used to."

Kelly didn't understand. "Used to what?"

"Live here."

Pain shot through her chest and down her arms. *Please don't kick us out. My kids...* "I don't understand this."

Kaitlin's eyes blazed with anger. "You said you were going to move out to get away from us."

"We have nowhere to go."

Kaitlin said, "We're painfully aware of that."

157

Jeremy shook his head as he stared at her. "Be thankful your sister has more compassion than you do. We signed a six-month lease on an apartment for the two of us. When that ends, you'd best be gone from here or I will kick you out. Understood?"

This couldn't be happening. "No Jeremy, you can't. I need the two of you. Katie, please..."

Kaitlin turned to her. "I hate you. Sorry you're my sister," She grabbed her husband's hand and the pair mounted the stairs.

Kelly's mouth was dry. She tried to talk, but no words came out. Kelly wanted to run upstairs, but her chest... She lowered herself to the bottom stair. *Please God. I screwed up. Please help me.*

The world was hazy. Kelly could hear them talking to her parents at the top of the stairs, but she didn't have the energy to even turn and watch them.

Kaitlin's voice was gentle as she spoke with Nora and Stan. "Daddy, we can't stay here, not after today. It's only temporary. Forgive us, but it's what we have to do. We have to watch out for us, and the baby."

"W-we understand," Stan's voice cracked.

"Are you sure there's no way you two girls can talk this out?" Nora pleaded.

"Not after what she did, Momma. For my sanity, I've got to go."

"Kelly made a mistake."

"Kelly almost destroyed my marriage."

"She's your sister."

"Not anymore. Not like she used to be. Good night."

Kelly heard the doors close upstairs. No one slept that night.

Chapter 31

The plumeria candle scented the room as Kelly walked into Martina's home for the weekly Sunday meal. The family was quite subdued. Jeremy and Kaitlin weren't there. When the doorbell rang, she hoped it was them. Her spirits tumbled when Cassandra walked in.

"What are you doing here, Cassie?"

Her sister hugged her for a long time. "I flew in to be here for you."

She wouldn't be able to get around it. It was coming. She wished Kaitlin had come, too.

When the dishes were put away and the kids were watching a movie, the core of the family moved into the kitchen. Martina cleared her throat. "Kelly, we know your life has been hard for the last year or so."

Kelly answered, "I'm fine, just fine. This isn't necessary."

Cassandra held her hand. "Liar! Tell us about it, Kelly."

I hate that word! Anger rose in Kelly, but her father walked over and cradled her in his arms. His touch softened her emotions. Frustration, anger, jealousy, hopelessness. They were what had driven her over the edge. But Daddy's arms soothed her, calmed her down. Just like when she was a little girl, his touch comforted her. His voice was calm and low as he whispered into her ear, "It's okay. You're surrounded by love."

Over the next two hours, Kelly revealed everything, including what had happened the previous day.

She apologized for driving a wedge in the family, but Nora comforted her. "Kaitlin will come around, in time. Right now's just too soon. She loves you. It'll be all right someday."

The family discussed her anger issues, suggesting Kelly seek professional help to control them.

"I can't afford that," Kelly said. "My medical coverage doesn't start for another month."

Martina patted her shoulder. "Don't worry. Anything you want or need, say the word and it's yours."

Cassandra kissed her sister's cheek. "That's right. And we're not only talking about money. You need a comforting ear or a shoulder to cry on, we'll be there. You should know we love you."

"But..."

"Family's everything," her mother replied. "We'll always be here."

I'm not worthy of this. Not after what I did to Katie. One thought nagged at her, the possible solution. She had to talk this out. "What happens if I decide I don't want this child?"

Silence greeted her. Cassandra spoke first. "We could talk about adoption if—"

"Suppose I want an abortion instead?" As soon as she verbalized it, she knew she wouldn't ever go through with it. Inside her, a young life was growing.

Her father's eyes were vacant as he answered, "I believe you know how we feel about abortion, but you're our daughter. You'll always be supported and loved unconditionally. Is that what you want to do?"

Every eye was fixated on her. "No. I couldn't ever do that."

The family breathed a collective sigh of relief. They advised her to see an obstetrician very soon. She agreed.

After hours of close discussion, they finished. Kelly again apologized, but instead of criticism she was met with hugs, kisses, words of comfort, and undeniable love. This was exactly what she had needed. But it tore her heart out that Kaitlin wasn't there. The hurt she had dumped on her sister and closest friend had been the cruelest thing she'd ever done. She'd give everything she owned to redo the previous day.

The family left. Kelly and her brood returned to the house Kaitlin and Jeremy owned. After bath time, prayers, and tucking in her children, Kelly wandered into the room where Kaitlin and Jeremy used to sleep. Holding her sister's pillow, she breathed in Kaitlin's perfume. With glistening eyes, she softly whispered, "I'm sorry. I miss you so much. You're more than a sister, you're my best friend. I love you."

That week, as promised, she saw both a psychiatrist and an obstetrician. The visit with the psychiatrist resulted in numerous prescriptions for depression medication and biweekly therapy.

At the obstetrician, a nurse led her into an examination room, and handed her a gown. The faint scent of bleach and industrial fabric softener emanated from the cloth. As the doctor examined her, she heard happy, laughing voices in the next treatment room. Quickly she realized those voices belonged to Jeremy and Kaitlin. *What are the chances we'd have appointments at the same time... at the same office?*

As she was leaving, Kaitlin and Jeremy walked out. The sisters stared at each other for a moment while Jeremy made the next appointment. Kelly started to walk toward her, but Kaitlin turned away. Jeremy didn't even acknowledge her.

***

His hands were shaking as he read the text. Geeter hadn't communicated with Kelly in quite a while. He was surprised when she texted, asking if they could Skype that night. Geeter texted back he was pretty tired but could possibly do the next evening.

The real reason Geeter didn't want to Skype had nothing to do with him being tired. True, he was exhausted, but he needed to mentally prepare himself. Since leaving Chicago, he had been trying to get over her, but failed miserably. She was everywhere. As he drove his Challenger or pickup, if he looked quickly, she was there on the seat next to him. He talked out loud to her constantly. *I'm losing my mind.*

To get over her, he picked up a girl at a bar in town, but when he leaned in to kiss her, it was Kelly's face he saw. Apologizing, he dropped her off at the curb in front of her house. Thoughts of Kelly filled his mind when he was awake and while he slept. He loved her so much, but it was one sided. That's why he'd been avoiding her. Now he'd have to bolster his courage, put on a good front. He decided to be kind, but distant. While part of him never wanted to speak with her again, the bigger part wouldn't let any opportunity to talk with her pass.

The following night, at the appointed time, Geeter's phone rang. Debating whether he could do it without breaking down, he finally answered on the fourth ring. As soon as Kelly's face filled his screen, he sensed something was very wrong. Her beauty shocked him... she was even more beautiful than he remembered, but something concerned him. She'd lost weight, and her cheekbones were more defined than when he had seen her last.

"Geeter, I've missed you so much!"

"Missed you, too, Kelly. How you been?"

That question opened the floodgates. He listened without saying a word. She talked about her children,

Kelly's parents and her work. She looked away and grew silent.

"What's wrong, Kelly?"

"Geeter, I don't know how to say this, but I'm pregnant."

Chills ran up his spine. *What? Could the child be mine?* She didn't mention who the father was, but he kept silent and listened as she talked.

"I had this horrible fight with Kaitlin. I don't know what took control of me."

When she described the argument, it came out she didn't know who the father was. How many men had she slept with? They had used protection, so the child couldn't be his. His heart broke in two. He would never be a father. He'd never love again.

His mind wandered. If the child was his, would that have made a difference? The sadness of talking with the girl he loved, but would never hold, was heart-wrenching. Kelly's question brought him back to the present.

"Are you all right?"

"Sure, why?"

"The screen's bouncing up and down."

"Sorry 'bout that. Just a little tired. Been working sixteen hours a day getting ready for planting. Pretty hard work," he lied.

He studied her face, amazed at her beauty. In his eyes, he could see her frustration grow, could hear it in her voice. She began to cry.

Geeter asked, "Did I do something to upset you?"

"No, not at all. It's just with this thing that happened with Katie, I feel like I lost my best friend."

"Know what it feels like."

"What do you mean?"

Oh crap! He hesitated until she asked him a second time. "Well, you know, there for a while we were pretty close. But then we drifted apart."

163

She wiped her eyes. "Sorry about that. With everything that happened, I didn't have time or energy to put into our friendship. But if you don't mind, I'd like to start over again."

Did I hear her right? "In what way?"

Kelly hesitated for a few seconds. "Friends, Geeter, just friends. I don't want any more than that. I really need your friendship, but if you don't want that, I understand. I seem to have a way of driving away the people I care about these days." Kelly swallowed hard and kept biting her lips.

Geeter knew she was fighting hard to maintain her composure. His heart was touched with empathy. What Geeter had been through during the past several weeks had hurt him. But was he ready to just be friends with the girl he loved? What would happen if he couldn't handle it? Was it worth going through the heartbreak again? "I, uh, I don't know Kelly."

She sniffed loudly, wiping her eyes. "I understand. I need to go now. Good night and goodbye."

Don't be so damned self-centered. I've gotta forget my fears. This girl he loved needed him, and even if it wasn't how he wanted it to be, he needed to be there for her.

"Don't go, Kelly. I'll be totally honest. When I left, my heart was broken. I shouldn't tell you this, but I was in love with you. Losing you almost killed me. I felt like I was dying."

She stared at the screen for several moments. "I'm sorry. Please realize I don't want anything more than friendship..."

"I h-heard y-you," his voice cracked. "I can't help it. I love you. But if just being friends is what you need, I'll be there for you. I may go crazy once in a while, but I'll try to be the friend you need."

Her voice was also breaking. "But Geeter..."

The pain in his heart was immense, but he refused to let her see it. "Don't want to talk about this no more. I told you I want to be your friend and I meant it."

Chapter 32

G eeter woke with a song in his heart the next day. Oddly enough, their call brought closure to his feelings. He knew exactly what Kelly wanted and needed—his friendship, not his love. He closed his mind to any chance of a loving relationship with Kelly.

That thought was on his mind when he stopped at the store for milk the next morning. Standing in line, he thought the cashier looked familiar. He smiled when he realized she was Becky Lee Jamison. Well, that had been her maiden name anyway. They hadn't dated in high school but had run around with the same group of friends. She had been very heavy-set back then. Not anymore. She looked trim and pretty. When the customer in front of him finished, Geeter said, "Hi, Becky, bet you don't remember me."

Becky's eyes crinkled when she smiled. "I do remember you. You're Geeter, right?"

He smiled in return. "Yep. My, you sure do look pretty!"

Becky blushed. "Thank you! Got tired of being fat and decided to do something about it. Lost ninety-five pounds and kept it off for ten years."

"Wow! That's great. What'cha been up to?"

"Not much, how 'bout you?" They chatted, quickly discovering they were both single.

The next man in line made it obvious he was in a hurry. In his New England accent, the tourist said, "Why don't you just save all of us some time and ask her out?"

Geeter turned, about to say something when Becky said quietly, "I think that's a great idea. Why don't you ask me out, Geeter?"

It was Geeter's turn to blush. Asking Becky out would be a great idea. *Why not?* "Wanna go out tonight?"

Merriment was evident in her smile. "Thought you'd never ask. I'd be honored."

The tourist sighed. "That took long enough! You people sure are slow!"

Hmmm. See how you like this. Geeter sat on the floor as he started removing his boots and socks.

The tourist yelled, "What in God's name are you doing?"

Geeter replied, "I only got ten fingers. Gonna need my toes to help count out what I owe!"

The tourist threw down his pack of gum and stormed out. Becky did her best not to laugh but failed miserably.

***

At the home in Oak Lawn, Kelly's life dragged on. She had come to understand how much Jeremy and Kaitlin had been doing for her. It was almost impossible to hold down a job, make meals, do the laundry, and take care of her children by herself. For the first time in over a year, she had to pump her own gas because Jeremy wasn't there to do it for her. Her parents helped, but their stamina wasn't what it used to be. She ended up hiring a full-time nanny to help, which Cassandra willingly paid for without question. But Kelly was miserable.

The sole bright spot in her life was Geeter and their talks. He didn't text like he used to, but he was there for her. They talked just about every other night following her shift. *Thank You, God, for sending him.* He was a great listener and friend.

"How's it going on the farm?" she'd ask.

"Oh, you know. Long days and hard work, but who's complainin'? Tell me about your day." That was exactly what she needed. Well, not really. She'd quickly come to the realization she wanted him. Her heart felt heavy when she recalled she'd said she only wanted friendship.

Valentine's Day was coming up. *Love... that's what it's all about.* The baby inside of her deserved love, deserved happiness. *I'll never find that with Todd.* Todd was most likely the father. Kelly trembled.

But Geeter. *He made me feel love.* The way he bonded with my children. *The way he made me feel. I've got to try.*

Kelly asked Geeter if they could talk after her shift. *She told him she had something to share with him.* Her heart was ready to burst from her chest. She'd decided to tell him she wanted more than friendship. He'd agreed to call after her shift, and Kelly couldn't wait.

Kelly stood naked in front of the bathroom mirror. She was starting to show, somewhat prominently. *Figures. Probably carrying triplets.* Seeing the belly bump against her very trim body deepened her depression. She needed to discuss this with her psychiatrist.

Kelly's heart wasn't whole, either. She missed Kaitlin. She tried to call her, but her sister didn't answer.

Later, Kaitlin texted back, "This an emergency?"

"No, but I want to straighten things out," Kelly replied.

"Maybe someday, but not now," came the cold response.

Valentine's Day dawned to find Kelly helping the nanny with the chores. She checked the mail, hoping

Geeter had mailed her a card. He hadn't. She checked her e-mail and phone for texts from him, but there were none. When she got to work, she saw several vases of roses, but none of them were for her. Her shift dragged on endlessly.

She was so excited, waiting for the shift to end. She couldn't wait to tell Geeter she'd changed her mind. She realized she was in love with him and wanted to say it out loud.

Kelly was giving her report to the night shift charge nurse when the train whistle alarm sounded on her phone, indicating a text message. She was running late and suspected his text would say he was waiting. Finishing as quickly as she could, she rushed to her car to read it.

"Kelly, sorry but can't talk tonight. Something came up. Happy Valentine's Day. See ya."

She stared at her phone. Why couldn't he talk? She suddenly understood. *I'm kidding myself.* I told him I didn't want him. This is my payback.

***

In Chattanooga, Geeter was sitting on Becky's love seat. His heart was beating loud enough to drown out a rock band. Becky's eyes glistened when she laughed at his jokes. Their first date had been so much fun, they agreed to a second date. That date led to a third, and when Geeter asked her out on Valentine's Day, Becky readily agreed. But instead of going out, Becky cooked chicken and dumplings for them. As they ate, Geeter kept checking his watch because he wanted to keep his date with Kelly.

Becky noticed his interest in the time. "Have somewhere else you need to be, Geeter?"

He glanced at Becky. *What the heck am I doing?* Kelly made it plain she only wanted friendship. *Becky's right here.* They had only just started, but something very special seemed to be happening between them.

Geeter smiled warmly. "Actually, I was supposed to talk to an old friend a little later tonight, but know what? I'm gonna cancel."

Becky looked disappointed. "Don't do that. If there's somewhere else you want to be, it's okay. I understand."

His smile covered his face. "Oh no, Becky. I want to be here, with you. Excuse me for a sec while I send a text, then I'm yours for the rest of the night, 'kay?"

Her disappointment turned into a warm smile. Five minutes later she set the table with hot apple pie and ice cream.

It was after one in the morning when Geeter left, but not before they shared their first kiss. Geeter realized he was truly happy for the first time in weeks.

***

Back at her parent's home, Kelly walked through the partially empty house. Everyone was in bed. The house was completely quiet. Once again, she stepped into the room Kaitlin and Jeremy once occupied. Climbing beneath their covers, she hugged Kaitlin's pillow. Kaitlin's fragrance still graced it. *I'm so lonely. So much I regret.* Which was the biggest disappointment, her cruelty to Kaitlin or telling Geeter she only wanted to be friends? That was a tossup. What was he doing? Had he found another girl? Was canceling tonight's call in retribution for saying she only wanted friendship? She needed to talk to Kaitlin, but it was too late and besides, Katie probably wouldn't answer anyway.

Kelly thought back to the night in New York when she and Geeter had made love. The whole day had been special. The camaraderie the two had shared turned her on so much. The easy conversation, the little teasing jokes, the smiles and the feel of his hand in hers had been so wonderful, so natural, as if God intended them to be together. And when they were at the Rockefeller Tree, Geeter had wrapped her in his arms. It was perfect. As he held her, she decided she wanted to make love with him.

It had actually taken some convincing on her part back in her room, not because he didn't want her, but because he tried to be so kind. He kept telling her they didn't have to do it because he didn't want a one-night stand. She hadn't seen lust in his eyes... no, it had been something more. On that special night, she'd seen love in his eyes.

Shivering under the covers, she chided herself for not realizing that everything she wanted had been right there in front of her. Like a fool she'd let it slip through her fingers. No, she'd thrown him away like a piece of trash. The love Geeter had given her was everything she needed in life. She fell asleep, dreaming of his embrace.

Chapter 33

The loud and obnoxious sound of a fire alarm filled the air. Kelly panicked, trying to orient herself. But she was in her bedroom. The alarm was only her cell's ring. She glanced at the clock. Seven thirty. "Hello?"

The voice on the other end exuded happiness. "Morning, Kelly. Wanted to apologize about not keeping our time together last night. I've got something important to tell you."

Her entire body warmed from the sound of his voice. "Geeter! I missed you. I was disappointed, but this call makes it all better. Can we Skype instead?"

"Sure. I'll hang up and call you right back."

When he came on the line, she could see he was in the barn. "Hey. Wanted to tell you 'bout last night. I met someone." Geeter told Kelly about meeting Becky and that he'd canceled because he was with her.

She gripped the mattress to keep from falling. *He looks so damned happy.*

He again apologized. "Becky and I've got a great connection. I know somethin' special's happening. You're my best friend, and I wanted to share it with you. Now, you had something to tell me. What was it?"

Bile filled her throat. She was going to throw up. The opportunity for love with Geeter had passed. Choking back tears, she somehow managed not to let her face show her disappointment. But what could she tell him? That she changed her mind? That she wanted to rekindle the romance they started? *Too late now.* It would be unfair to say it. Instead, she lied. "I forget what it was, but I'm sure I'll remember it later. I've got to get going now because the kids are up. Really happy for you. Goodbye." As soon as she disconnected, she buried her head in her pillow.

***

Todd stopped for a coffee at a convenience store before heading into the hospital. As soon as he entered, he caught a whiff of a fragrance. *Kelly.* Curious, he sauntered through the store looking for the origin of the scent. Disappointed in not finding it, he poured a coffee and stood in line. That's when he noticed her, right in front of him.

He'd thought of Kelly quite often, but seeing her now, he was again smitten with her beauty. But something about her was different. *What is it?* Was it his imagination, or did she have a little bit of a belly bump? His mouth dropped open. *She's pregnant.* He remembered the first time they'd made love. When he'd discovered the torn condom. That bulge might have been caused by him. He had to find out.

"Hi, Kelly! Remember me?"

As soon as she turned suddenly, her face flushed. *That good or bad?*

"Of course. How are you?"

"I'm fine. You look great. How have you been?" Now that she was facing him, he couldn't help but stare at her belly. She was showing!

She hesitated, as if she knew what he was staring at. "Actually, life has been a little tough lately."

He got right to the point. "I know I shouldn't ask this and forgive me if I am wrong, but are you pregnant?"

She blushed a crimson shade of red, jaws clamping together tightly. "Yes."

Now that Todd was certain, excitement filled his heart. *She's carrying my child!* He smiled broadly, then toned it down just a little. "Well, I guess we both know I'm the father."

Kelly's eyes lit up as if they were on fire. "Why would you automatically assume that?"

"You slept with me."

"Maybe I slept with somebody else." She looked infuriated. Two men in the other line struggled to get a good look at Kelly.

"Maybe you did, but I know something you don't know."

"What would that be?" Her voice was increasing in volume. Everyone in both lines was blatantly eavesdropping on the conversation now.

Want to draw attention? How's this? "Remember the first time we made love, and I became sad afterwards?"

Her face turned a deep shade of red. "What about it?"

"The reason I was sad was because the condom broke." Everyone in both lines no longer pretended to eavesdrop. They all turned away.

She screamed, "And you didn't think to tell me?" The mouths of several women in line dropped open.

He hesitated. "No, I was hoping nothing would happen. But since it did, I'm glad. You know, we can pick up right where we left off. I'm still in love with you, Kelly."

Kelly's lips turned into a tight white line. "Like hell! I'm not in love with you!"

One of the women in line yelled out, "Good for you, sister!"

Todd ignored the woman. His anger was building. She was carrying his child and that child belonged to him.

He tried a calmer approach. "Kelly, think about if we got together. You'd have a father for our child, someone to provide for you and our baby. You'll never have to want for anything, ever again!"

She snarled, "Quit referring to my baby as ours. There is no way I want anything to do with you!"

Anger settled like an avalanche over him. "Better reconsider. I will be part of our baby's life, even if I have to take you to court. Are you seeing an obstetrician?"

"That's none of your damn business! Get away from me!" She started to walk away, but he grabbed her arm, turning her violently toward him. Two construction workers in the other line set their purchases down and started to come to Kelly's rescue. They needn't have bothered.

"I won't let you alone. Come on, Kelly! Think of our baby."

Kelly threw her hot coffee at his chest. "It's my baby, not yours! Stay away from me, or I'll call the police."

The hot fluid burned, but he pulled his shirt away from his chest. Todd glared at her. "That child is mine. I'll do whatever I have to do to be part of our son or daughter's life."

She threw her empty cup at him as she backed away. "Then take me to court after the baby's born. Don't be surprised to find out it isn't your child!"

What? You slept with someone else? He started to follow her. "Who's the father? Answer that for me."

She turned, walking away. Over her shoulder, she tossed, "Screw you, Andrews."

He smiled, yelling after her, "You already did. Careful now. You're carrying my child."

He turned around to discover everyone staring at him. The man behind him said, "You're a real jackass." Todd laughed, then threw a ten on the counter and left.

Chapter 34

K elly was seething after the encounter with Todd. Somehow she made it through her shift, but it was difficult. What he said was on her mind. Most likely, he was the baby's father.

She didn't want him as a partner, husband, or anything else though. The encounter in the convenience store once again validated her feelings. Even if he was the last man on earth, she'd never be with him again. He wanted control. If they did become a couple, what would it be like in ten years or thirty? He would tell her what to wear, what to say, what to do. Screw that! She'd rather be a nun than put up with him!

Kelly drove home, but her mind drifted back to Geeter. What would it be like with him in ten, twenty or thirty years? Her lip hurt as she bit it. *What did I do?* Our partnership would have been so special, so sweet. Their time together had been brief, but so incredible. And she'd blown it. She'd regret telling him she only wanted to be friends. Regret it until she drew her last breath.

Her nerves were shot. Before going into the house, she texted Kaitlin, "I need help. Can we talk, please?"

Kaitlin's response came back, "Is it an emergency? Are you in danger?"

Kelly texted, "No, but my world's upside down. I need you!" There was no response.

Two sleepless hours later, Kelly headed downstairs. Mindlessly staring at the television, she was having a pity party for herself. Rubbing her belly, she spoke to her unborn child. "I'm sorry your mom is so screwed up. I should be rejoicing because I'm carrying you. Mom's having a hard time right now. This is the lowest point in my life."

Just before she left for work the next afternoon, she discovered she was wrong. When the mailman knocked on the door for a signature on a certified letter, fear choked her. Her breathing was shallow. The letter was from Family Court. The judge had scheduled a hearing to consider Ballister's petition for joint custody.

"Par for the course," Kelly muttered bitterly as she dropped the letter on the counter. She had no one to talk to, so her unborn child became her captive audience, her only friend. "Baby, I think you're a little girl. If you are, I'm naming you Kaitlin Elizabeth, in honor of your aunt and my best friend. Maybe she'll forgive me someday."

The ache in her back was matched by the pounding in her head. Before leaving for work, she wrote down everything she felt in an e-mail. After a long prayer, she sent it to Kaitlin, but doubted her sister would respond.

Kelly and her baby went to work that evening. One problem seemed to cascade into another. She breathed in the cold night air two hours after her shift ended.

Her eyes were scratchy, her nose dripping. Before starting the car, she buried her head in her hands for a good long cry. She needed to tell the doctor her depression was increasing.

Studying the heavens, she prayed, *"God, I know You're listening. Please give me a positive sign."* As if God answered immediately, a brilliant shooting star cut a swath through the dark night. Kelly's heart lifted.

Arriving home, she discovered God had answered her prayers with not one, but two additional blessings. As she climbed into bed, she checked her text messages. Geeter had sent a long one telling her she was on his mind. He wanted to talk Saturday morning. This made her happy, yet sad. Geeter was a great friend, but again, she realized she was in love with him. She wiped her cheeks. Geeter would probably want to spend time with Becky on Saturday night, so she texted for him to call her at six Saturday morning, before the kids woke up.

She checked her mail account. Much to her surprise, an e-mail from Kaitlin was waiting. It read:

Kelly,

I'm sorry your life is so tough right now. I'm still hurt by what you did, but we're sisters, nothing will change that. Let's put this behind us.

If you want to bury the hatchet, let's do lunch on Saturday. (I'll drive this time, okay ☺?).

By the way, I'm carrying twin girls. We decided to name one Kelli Alexandra in honor of you. You're still my hero, did you know that? The other one will be named Megan Marie. Pick you up at twelve thirty. Jeremy can't wait to see you at the family lunch on Sunday.

Love, Katie

Kelly's eyes filled with tears of happiness, and for the first time in weeks, she slept soundly.

Her weekend was perfect. The talk with Geeter was like it used to be and lasted until almost nine. The meal with Kaitlin was filled with laughter. Their "lunch" lasted until five. Afterwards, they went baby shopping together.

On Sunday, Jeremy smiled. "I missed you, sis. Forgive us for not being there when you needed us."

Her response was choked. "Forgive me. All my fault, starting with the way I treated you. Also for lying to Kaitlin about you. And..."

He hugged her tightly, whispering in her ear, "It's all in the past. Don't know what you're talking about."

Kelly's heart was filled with joy.

After the lunch, the adults had another brief conference concerning strategy. Gary felt very comfortable the judge would rule in their favor. Kelly was reflective on the drive home with her parents, feeling happier than she had in months. The only two sad points were thoughts of the upcoming court date and the big one, which she knew would always make her cry—the sadness of letting Geeter go. The court date, three weeks from now, was one week before K.J.'s eighth birthday.

Chapter 35

T he furniture polish smell again greeted Kelly as she entered the courtroom, her parents bracketing her. Kaitlin, Jeremy and Martina followed, providing moral support. *Thank You for my family.*

Ballister entered shortly afterwards. He stopped in the aisle to stare at the belly bumps both Kelly and Kaitlin were sporting. He glared at Jeremy. "Knocked up both sisters, huh?"

Jeremy's fists clenched, but he didn't say a word. Ballister's lawyer grabbed his arm and yanked him toward his seat.

The case did not go well for her ex-husband. The court-appointed custodian reported Ballister ignored his three other children while focusing all of his attention on K.J. The former cop read everything he'd documented... every smart mouth and nasty comment Ballister uttered.

The judge returned from her chamber. "After careful consideration, we'll revisit the custody request in one year. Also, visitation rights are reduced to one hour every third week."

Ballister was fit to be tied as he walked out of the courtroom. He stopped in front of Kelly, whispering with malice, "You little slut! This ain't over by a long shot. You'll pay, I guarantee it."

***

K.J.'s eighth birthday started with the family—including Kaitlin and Jeremy who had moved home—waking him with a song. Kelly had taken off to celebrate his birthday and gave her son an extra-long hug when she dropped him off at school. The warm aroma of cake and the taste of sugary icing filled the kitchen as she baked and decorated a special cake for him.

The warmth of an unusually mild late-winter day caressed her in the car as Kelly waited at the school. But when the other children came out, K.J. wasn't there. *Something's wrong.* Worry reared its ugly head. Was K.J. sick or in trouble? She signed in at the office then walked to his classroom.

The smell of antiseptic soap and gum erasers greeted her. "Hi, Mrs. Baker. K.J. didn't come out. Everything okay?" Kelly glanced around the empty classroom. "Is he here?"

The teacher's face blanched. "No. His father picked him up at noon."

"What?" Kelly screamed.

"Yes," the teacher dug through her desk. She pulled a piece of paper out of a file, handing it to Kelly. "He said it was K.J.'s birthday and you gave him permission to take his son out someplace special for the day. His father gave me this note you signed to let K.J. out of school early."

Kelly grabbed the note. "This isn't my signature!" Kelly's heart pounded as if it would beat out of her chest. K.J.'s teacher grabbed her hand as they ran to the office. The principal immediately called the police. Kelly was hyperventilating as she sent a group text to her family stating Ballister had kidnapped K.J.

Chapter 36

The glow of the neon light seemed to soothe Ballister, or maybe it was the whiskey chaser. He needed it after the disaster in court.

"It's all her fault." Sure, he'd made a mistake leaving her and the kids for that stupid actress, but still, it had only been a mid-life crisis. Couldn't she understand that?

The bartender poured another shot. "You all right?"

Ballister liked the way the alcohol vapors tickled his nose. "She could have made everything right. Instead, she got knocked up."

"Sorry to hear that."

"Yeah, my life sucks. Know who I was married to?"

The bartender was drying a glass. "Who?"

"Sherrie Sanford. You know, the actress?"

The bartender studied his face. "She's pregnant?"

The pounding in his head increased. "No, my first wife. Left her for Sherrie."

"Sherrie Sanford is one hot actress. Remember that movie where she did the wild group love scene? Let me tell you..."

"Shut up!" The bartender's face seemed to pulse as a spasm hit Ballister's left eye. "That's my wife. Well... ex-wife."

"Sorry." The barkeep moved to another patron.

Ballister's mind went back to when he'd met Sherrie. She was a new patient, there for a consult. So much prettier in person than on the screen. He couldn't help but fantasize about her. She picked up on it, and to his surprise, she made his fantasy a reality right there in the treatment room. That had been the beginning of it all—a hot and steamy affair. She introduced him to an erotic and promiscuous world he never dreamed existed.

Sherrie quickly became jealous of Kelly, begging him to leave his wife for her. Sherrie promised him a life of luxury and unlimited sexual adventure. Ballister's mind was consumed by lust for her.

Shaking his head, he motioned for another hit of Jack Daniels. He'd been suffering from severe headaches for a couple of months before he met Sherrie. When all this went down, he didn't even wonder why he fell for her. He knew why, now. *Too late.*

When he married Sherrie, he thought she'd be faithful to him. *Yeah, right.* The day after their honeymoon was over, he came home to find out she wasn't. He threw a tantrum, which turned into a knockdown, drag out fight. The fight turned physical, and when he punched her, that damned bodyguard forcibly threw him out. Sherrie filed for divorce a mere eight days after their wedding.

The clinking of glass tapping against glass caught his attention. His shot glass rattled against the beer bottle. *Great. The shakes have returned.* His pride wouldn't let him contact Kelly or the kids. But as the loneliness of Christmas approached, he realized he wanted his marriage back. Christmas Day was the perfect time to start over. What a wonderful gift for Kelly and his children—to restore the family. To get back what was rightfully his. But no. *Bitch!* She'd refused.

The barkeep plopped another longneck down. Ballister slowly peeled the label. He wanted what was his, but her family had stuck their big fat noses in his business. Especially that SOB Jeremy. The shaking was subsiding. Kelly's face appeared before him in the reflection of the bottle. "The bullcrap they feed you is the reason you won't take me back." That had to be the only reason. Jeremy and Kaitlin had brainwashed the twins. Kelly Junior was the only one who cared for him at all.

The bartender returned with another shot of whiskey. "Last one, bud. Here's your tab." Ballister lifted the glass, studying it. His mind drifted back to the debacle in the courtroom. His wife, his own wife, was pregnant. He knew right away Jeremy had fathered that child. The woman with whom he shared ten years of his life had turned out to be a tramp, just like Sherrie.

Doesn't matter anyway. The day after court, his head hurt so badly, he'd broken down and seen a doctor. *Wish I hadn't.* Within a day, they'd diagnosed the problem. And ended his life. The doctor came in with the saddest face.

"Mr. Ballister, I have the results of the tests."

"Why do I have such a bad headache?"

"I'm sorry, Mr. Ballister."

"Don't keep me in suspense."

"Have you noticed a change in your decision-making in the last few months?"

"What?" He thought back to his decision to leave Kelly for Sherrie.

"I'll get right to the point. You have an inoperable brain tumor in the ventral prefrontal cortex. Patients similarly diagnosed show a propensity to make—"

"Wait! You said it's inoperable, right?"

"Yes. I'm sorry."

Ballister nodded. *"How long do I have?"*

"Hard to tell. Patients with inoperable tumors of this size usually are looking at a short span, say one to

three months. There are a variety of other options available, such as chemo."

"What's the success rate?"

"Low unfortunately, however, with the improvements..."

He listened to the doctor. The long and short of it was, the likelihood of a recovery was slight, and his quality of life wouldn't be very good during treatment. Ballister decided to let nature ride out its course. He had a few things he wanted to do.

One good thing about it. He would be able to pay quite a few people back for ruining his life without spending eternity in a jail cell.

Ballister grimaced. "My life's over. I'll never know happiness again." He finished off the beer. "If I can't have happiness, no one else will either. Payback's a bitch. No one will live out a fairy tale in this family." He downed the shot of whiskey, slapped a couple twenty-dollar bills on the bar and staggered out to meet his destiny.

Chapter 37

K elly wiped her mouth, the taste of vomit lingering. Looking up, Kaitlin and Jeremy were by her side. She was struggling to maintain her sanity. Kelly's chest was pounding so badly she feared it would affect the baby. Kelly clung tightly to her sister. Martina arrived a few moments later.

Martina squeezed her hand. "Gary went to the house. Your children and mom and dad are safe."

A man in a heavy navy coat walked in. "Looking for Ms. Jenkins."

Martina replied, "She's here."

"Name's Miller. Detective Dick Miller. Your son missing?"

Kelly could only nod. After the detective finished with her, he interviewed K.J.'s teacher and the principal. Kelly recalled her ex-husband's threat and told the police. CPD offered to provide a squad car for protection.

"That won't be necessary," Martina spoke up. "She'll be staying with me. My husband made arrangements for private security. We have an elaborate alarm system, and the security professionals are armed—former Navy SEALs. Everyone will be well protected."

It was almost eight when they left the school. Kelly rode in Martina's BMW SUV, while Jeremy and Kaitlin followed in his truck. Martina patted her hand. "CPD issued an arrest warrant for Ballister. They'll find him."

Kelly nodded. It was hard to be strong. When they passed a Department of Transportation sign, she lost it. It showed an Amber Alert for her son.

***

Geeter's head was swimming. He and Becky had grown very close. Even though he spoke frequently with Kelly, he spent his time with Becky. He was moved, seeing how understanding and supportive she was, especially considering Becky knew about Kelly and understood there was a remote possibility the child she was carrying might be his.

Both of them agreed they wanted a long-term relationship but decided to take it slow. Geeter still smarted over Kelly's rejection and Becky was upset about her ex-husband. Just when everything had seemed perfect, he'd suddenly fallen out of love with her after nine years of marriage.

The enticing smell of brick oven pizza had Geeter salivating. They were at a pizza parlor when Jeremy's number came up on Geeter's cell phone. Looking at Becky, he smiled. "It's my old L.T. from my Army days. I'll put it on speaker so I can introduce you." She smiled. "Hey, L.T.! What's cooking?"

"Geeter, Ballister kidnapped K.J."

Geeter immediately took the phone off speaker. Everything in the room took on a red tint. "What? When did this happen? Kelly okay?"

"Today. Took him from school today. It's K.J.'s birthday."

Geeter was trembling. "Damn that man! How's Kelly holding up?"

"Not very well at all. She's having chest pain, and her nerves are shot. Don't know if you know this or not, but after court, he threatened her."

He glanced at Becky. She was staring at him with a worried look on her face.

Geeter suddenly had a severe headache. He rubbed his temple. "I know. She told me about it. Think he's serious?"

"The police do. Kelly's staying at Martina's home. With their security system and the private security they hired, they're protected."

"Okay. Give me orders. What can I do?"

"Nothing, except pray the police find him quickly and that K.J. is okay."

"Think I should call Kelly now?"

"Now probably isn't a good time. Call her tomorrow."

"I will. Thanks for letting me know, and if there is anything... anything at all, I can do... tell Kelly to let me know. Nothing in the world could be more important than that!"

"I will, buddy. Just pray for both of them."

Geeter hung up.

Becky smiled sadly. "I know you still care deeply for her. Go, if for no other reason than moral support."

The pounding in his head was getting worse. Geeter stared at her. She knew his true feelings for Kelly but was so supportive. "Will you go with me, Becky?"

Her shoulders slumped forward. "I can't just leave work. Your friend needs you. Let's get out of here so you can book a flight."

He drove Becky home and kissed her good night. She asked him to call her when he arrived. He kissed her again and left. In the darkness, Becky waved goodbye. He booked a 7:00 A.M. flight from Chattanooga to O'Hare.

***

Jeremy and Kaitlin arrived at Martina's house in the morning. The Navy SEALs met them at the door. Even though they recognized him, they frisked Jeremy.

After a brief conversation, Kelly said she wanted to go home to gather clothes and supplies for her family.

One of the SEALs said, "I'll accompany you, Ms. Jenkins."

Gary shook his head. "The children and my in-laws are here. Jeremy is an ex-Ranger. He can easily handle Ballister if they run into him at their house."

Jeremy's eyes narrowed. "If I could only be that lucky."

The SEAL shrugged his shoulders. "You're the boss, Mr. Davis." He turned to Jeremy. "I think you should go and return as soon as possible."

Jeremy nodded. "I'll be careful." He turned to Kaitlin and said, "Stay here."

Kaitlin's eyes opened wide. "Get it through your thick skull. Where you go, I go."

"Katie, you're pregnant."

"And so are you, I mean... you're expecting. Oh, whatever. I'm coming."

"I would really prefer you to stay here."

"Leave me here and I'll just follow behind you. I'd feel better if I were with you."

Kelly nodded in the direction of the SEALs. "Maybe one of these guys should take me."

Jeremy shot a look at Kaitlin that let her know they would talk about it later. Kaitlin slowly smiled. "Let's go."

***

Geeter arrived at the Davis home. Gary invited him in and took him to see the children. The girls clung to him and the baby smiled as he pulled Geeter's hair.

After he broke away, Martina patted his shoulder. "Good to see you again. Kaitlin and Jeremy took her over to the house to get clothes for the children. You can wait here if you want."

Geeter wanted to see Kelly so badly, it hurt inside. She'd need him. Geeter fumbled with the rental keys and looked Martina steadily in the eyes. "No 'fense, but I didn't come all the way up north just to sit an' wait. I'll go meet 'em there."

Chapter 38

B allister slapped a half dozen acetaminophen tablets in his mouth, chasing them with water. He was parked two blocks away, keeping watch on the Roberts' home with binoculars. His son K.J. was sitting beside him staring listlessly out of the window. Ballister had spiked his son's orange juice with vodka at breakfast so K.J. wouldn't have a clue about what was going on. Ballister knew this was the end of his journey. One last scene. Revenge was on the menu. And he was the waiter.

When a police car drove by, he scrunched down in the seat so he wouldn't be seen. *Good thing I switched cars.* A week's worth of planning was about to pay off. Paybacks were a bitch, and he couldn't wait. He'd watched Jeremy and Kaitlin leave earlier, banking on them returning with Kelly. *Damn, I'm good.* He was right!

Ballister waited ten minutes after they entered before taking K.J. out of the van. Dragging his son to the porch, he rang the bell. While he waited, he pulled a nine-millimeter semi-automatic pistol from his coat, pointing it at K.J.'s head. The firmness of the cold steel gave him courage.

Jeremy came to the door and looked through the window.

Ballister called out, "Open up or I'll shoot him."

Jeremy hesitated for a few seconds before complying.

Dragging his son into the living room, Ballister ordered Jeremy to stand with his back against the wall in front of the fireplace. Kelly and Kaitlin came down the stairs carrying clothes for the children. As they reached the bottom, Kelly gasped. Ballister felt a smile curl his lips.

"Hey, bitches!" he chuckled. "Miss me?" He waved his pistol at them. "Get your fat bellies over there next to your lover."

The women walked across the room to where Jeremy stood. When Kelly was closest to K.J., she reached for her son. Ballister swung the pistol, hitting her across the cheekbone hard enough to draw blood. She collapsed.

Jeremy twisted around to make a move, but Ballister leveled the pistol at him. "One more inch, and you get it first! Nothing I'd love more. Don't make me do it out of turn!"

Jeremy backed off, raising his hands. Kaitlin helped her sister to her feet then Jeremy gently guided them to stand behind him. Ballister smiled.

"Isn't this just precious? The three who did me in. So Jeremy, tell me. Did you knock them both up at the same time?"

Kelly's eyes narrowed. "He's not the father of my child, you idiot! Leave him alone."

A sudden spasm caused him to shake. "Aww! Katie, do you see how protective your sister is of your husband? How does that make you feel? I mean, knowing he screwed your sister and fathered her child, too?"

"You're so vile," Kaitlin answered. "What do you want? What do we have to do to get you out of our lives?"

He sneered at her. "What do I want? Well, that's easy. I want what's rightfully mine! I want my children back. I want my wife back..."

"You threw us away like we were nothing," Kelly yelled. "You had it all, but you ditched the kids and me for that damn actress. What happened between you anyway?"

The pounding in Ballister's head affected his vision. The faces of his captives were blurry. But not blurry enough to miss Jeremy's eyes assessing the scene. Mr. ex-Army hot shot was obviously looking for an opportunity to strike. *Hope you try it, asshole.* Ballister was far enough away that he could easily shoot him if he lunged. Yep, Jeremy would get it first if he tried anything. Even though Ballister was bantering with the girls, his eyes followed Jeremy. *You're the real threat, Mr. Tougher-than-shit ex-Army Ranger, not the girls.*

"The bitch used me. She only wanted me because I was taken. As soon as we married, she dumped me."

Jeremy joined the verbal fray. "You never referred to women like you just did. Why start now?"

Ballister's eyes lit up. "Because they're no better than dogs. Look how Sherrie used me. Kelly is a real dog because she couldn't wait to sleep with you. And what happened? You knocked her up. Nothing but a common whore. And your wife Katie? Stupid as a mutt. Look who she married."

Jeremy's voice lowered. "For the last several months, I watched you invest all your time with K.J."

That nickname made Ballister so angry he spit at Jeremy. He started shaking violently. "His name is 'Kelly Junior'!"

Jeremy held his hands in front of him. "My apologies. For the last several months, you invested all your time in Kelly Junior, ignoring your other children and showering him with love. Now, you have a gun on him. Why?"

"That's simple! I thought if there was any hope that one of my children would ever understand me and be on my side, it was Kelly Junior. But your nosy, controlling, useless family has him wrapped around your little finger so tightly, there's absolutely no hope even he'd ever understand me. And the way my ex-wife stuck it to me in court? I'll never have custody of my children. My life is over, and you three are the ones I can thank for that."

Kelly was applying direct pressure to the wound on her cheek. "Let our son go, please?"

Ballister laughed.

"What the hell do you want?" Kelly screamed.

He was enjoying this. "Revenge, my dear, revenge."

"What's that supposed to mean? Revenge for what? You brought all your problems on by yourself!"

"Think what you want. I'll never be happy again, so the best thing I can do is make sure none of you will ever be, either." He smiled bitterly at Jeremy. "Let's start with the child my wife is carrying. Your child. In just a few minutes, I'll take care of the worthless kid, followed quickly by the man who slept with her. And then it will be sweet little Katie's turn." His eyes narrowed as he glared at Jeremy. "I know you fathered her child. Kelly has always liked you. Has since she met you. I just never thought you'd do it. So, tit for tat. But it's my turn now. Me and Katie."

Before Jeremy could answer or move, a strange voice with a distinct Southern accent drifted in from the doorway. "Got it all wrong, Bubba. That child ain't his, it's mine."

Chapter 39

S ince Geeter had just missed Kelly when he arrived at Martina's house, he stopped at a florist to buy a bouquet of flowers, hoping they might take Kelly's mind off the situation, if even for a few seconds.

Geeter turned the corner to Jeremy and Kaitlin's house just in time to see a man dragging K.J. up the porch steps. Even from a distance, he recognized him. It was Ballister. He had seen the scumbag in court. He immediately called 911. Kelly's ex was small and no match for Jeremy, but when the man pulled a weapon from his coat pocket and aimed it at K.J.'s head, Geeter sprang into action.

He parked his rental car further down the street and waited until they entered the house before running to the porch. Quietly, he tried the door. Jeremy had left it unlocked. The brass knob was cold as he slowly swung the door inward, praying the hinges wouldn't squeak.

On high alert, Geeter silently listened. Positioning himself where he could keep an eye on the street, he planned on directing the police inside. Every nerve in his body was on fire. If things went downhill, he was ready.

At once he heard Kelly scream, followed by Ballister saying, "Revenge, my dear, revenge." Geeter surveyed the situation through the crack in the doorway. Kelly's ex was positioned with his back to a wall in the center of the room. The girls were standing behind Jeremy. Ballister's attention was fully on the ex-Ranger.

Geeter came up with a plan. He would draw the man's attention so Jeremy could widen the angle between them. He prayed Jeremy would remember the incident in Basra, Iraq—one he and Jeremy resolved.

Ballister had just finished saying Kaitlin would get it last when Geeter couldn't take it anymore. "Got it all wrong, Bubba. That child ain't his, it's mine."

Ballister backed against the wall, pulling his son closer.

Geeter's senses were on full alert, just like they'd been on the battlefield. The scent of pine, the shine from the polished floor, the blood on Kelly's cheek. He turned his eyes to the man with the gun. Ballister was no dummy. He was watching both of them, eyes darting back and forth as he tried to comprehend the situation. It was obvious Geeter was spoiling Ballister's plan.

Geeter's eyes didn't leave the gun. "Hey, Captain Roberts. Kind of reminds you of that day in the command center in Basra, doesn't it?" He hoped both Jeremy's mind and feet were swift.

"Sure does, Staff Sergeant Smith," Jeremy replied.

What I wanted to hear. He motioned to Kelly. "Come over here and stand behind me, Sugar Britches."

Ballister appeared to be confused, probably not knowing who Geeter was or how much of a threat he might be. No doubt Ballister hadn't noticed him in the courtroom.

"Kelly, that's a great idea," Jeremy said. "Go stand behind Gideon."

"Gideon? Who the hell are you?" Ballister stared at Geeter in disbelief.

Kelly ran behind Geeter so quickly her ex didn't have a chance to do anything. Jeremy moved to his right, which extended the angle, making sure to keep Kaitlin behind him.

"Me? Aw, hell, I ain't nobody. Not since I left the Rangers. But in Iraq, they called me Gideon, the Angel of Death. Now, 'fore something really bad happens, let the boy go. Be awful friendly if you dropped the gun, too."

Ballister didn't seem to know what to do. He hissed, "Get out of this house unless you want to die. You're spoiling my plan, but I have more than enough bullets to shoot you, too!"

Geeter shook his head as he took a step toward Ballister, widening his own angle. Across the room, Jeremy was also sidestepping. "Wanna git to her? Gotta go through me first."

"Gig's up, Ballister," Jeremy called. "You're outmanned."

Ballister's head turned from side to side as he tried to watch both of them. The sound of approaching police sirens caused his head to jerk toward the door.

Geeter used his most menacing voice. "You hear 'em? They're comin' for you, son. They gonna shoot you like a possum. Now, let the boy go, drop the gun, and no one gets hurt. We can all go home. You can't get away with this."

"Like hell I won't. Think you're both so smart?"

While he was looking at Geeter, Jeremy stepped forward. Ballister caught the movement and aimed the gun at Jeremy. "One more step and..." Jeremy took another step closer. "You want to die first? No problem!"

Geeter loudly whistled and stamped his foot, drawing Ballister's attention. Jeremy started to lunge forward. While Ballister may have been looking at Geeter, he again caught Jeremy's sudden movement. Pushing K.J. to the ground, Ballister whipped to his left to face Jeremy. He squeezed the trigger twice.

Jeremy's body dropped to the floor. Geeter immediately sprang forward.

With a fluid motion, Ballister spun, firing three shots point blank into Geeter's chest. From out of nowhere, a runaway train floored Geeter and kept on rolling.

***

The sirens were louder, as if they were right outside. Kaitlin grabbed Jeremy as he tumbled back toward her. His motionless body seemed to weigh a ton.

Ballister grabbed Kelly. "Not much time left. On your knees." He twisted her arm, forcing her to the floor. "Now, to eliminate your lover's child..."

"No!" Kelly screamed.

Rage exploded in Kaitlin. Her eyes narrowed at the gun pointed at her sister's belly. A heavy ceramic vase sat on the end table. The twin handles were cold as she lifted it over her head.

"Leave my sister alone!" she screamed. Rushing forward, she slammed the vase three times against Ballister's head before it broke.

He fell to his knees, but grabbed Kaitlin's arm, squeezing it violently. His breath was rapid and he used her for leverage to stand. The gun was nowhere in sight as he grasped her shoulder with the other hand.

Ballister's arms trembled, mildly at first, but it quickly escalated into uncontrollable shudders. He opened his mouth to say something, his grip loosened, and he crumpled to the floor, eyes staring listlessly at the ceiling.

The front door slammed against the wall, punching a hole in the drywall. "Police, drop your weapons," shouted one of two uniformed officers who burst into the room.

Noting Ballister's weapon on the floor, one of the officers stepped on it and kicked it away.

Kaitlin stared at Ballister's motionless body.

The second officer checked for a pulse. "This guy's dead. Check the other one." He pointed at Jeremy.

Jeremy! Oh my God. In horror, she watched the officer. "Still alive. Call a bus."

Kaitlin rushed to Jeremy's side, not knowing what to do. Blood was oozing out of his shirt. "Kelly!" she screamed, "What should I do! Tell me what to do!"

Kelly grabbed K.J., holding him tightly while staring at her ex-husband's body on the floor.

"Kelly! Help me!" Kaitlin's plea seemed to bring her out of her daze.

Turning to Kaitlin, she yelled back, "They said he has a pulse. Is he breathing?"

Kaitlin placed her ear near his mouth. "Yes."

"Check. Did the bullets go through and come out his back? Feel for holes."

Kaitlin rolled Jeremy's body to feel his back. "No. No holes."

"Apply direct pressure. Grab something and hold it over the wound."

Kaitlin grabbed a handful of children's clothes, holding them tightly over both his wounds. "Jeremy, stay with me!" she pleaded. "I need you. I love you. Don't give up on me! Your girls and I need you, baby!"

Kelly clung tightly to K.J. as she watched her sister. Kaitlin continued to plead as she held the cloth against her husband's chest.

The police officers were watching Kaitlin. "Hey. You check the other guy with the chest wounds yet?"

"Yeah. No pulse. He's gone. Let's check the rest of the house."

Kaitlin's head spun to her sister. Kelly's face turned white.

"No, God, no. He took the bullets meant for me!" The pool of blood around Geeter's body was staining the tan carpet. "Please. He can't be dead. Please, don't take him from me."

She kissed K.J. before kneeling in the pool of blood next to Geeter. She checked for a pulse.

"Geeter. Stay with me!" She hammered his chest and started CPR compressions. The trauma nurse in her seemed to come back online. Tears flowed freely from her eyes. *"God,"* she prayed out loud, *"please don't take him. If You never grant me another prayer, don't let him die, please God!"*

Chapter 40

G eeter's fingers were outstretched, ready to rip Ballister's weapon from him when the muzzle flashed once, twice, and a third time. Hot, searing lightning bolts ripped through his chest, with the impact of a tractor trailer speeding down on him. Suddenly, he was falling, slamming to the floor. Immediately, he jumped to his feet and again lunged at Ballister to protect Kelly, but he ran straight through Ballister. He turned in time to see Kaitlin smash the vase against Ballister's head. He stood helpless as the man grasped Kaitlin's arms before suddenly collapsing.

That's when Geeter saw it. His own body. On the floor. Motionless. Blood oozing from his chest. Eyes opened, staring toward heaven. He stood there in shock until startled by his mother's voice.

He turned in that direction, and there were his parents. Behind them stood their farmhouse. On the porch were so many people Geeter had known. They were all smiling. The front door was thrown wide open, and a brilliant light filtered out of the doorway. So appealing and pleasant. He was drawn to it.

His parents were smiling, and both reached their hands toward him. "Geeter, it's time to come home. Your time here is done. Your life's purpose has been fulfilled. It is time to receive your reward. It's time to meet Jesus."

The light was so warm and inviting. He stepped over his body and walked to his parents. Never had he known such joy! He hugged them and walked toward the door.

The smell of spring flowers and homebaked bread greeted him. He felt no pain, only happiness in his soul. His friends and relatives who had passed were all reaching out to him. Just before he reached the steps, a cool hand touched his chest, and little raindrops hit his face.

He stopped and turned toward his body. Kelly was kneeling next to him, depressing his chest. It should hurt, but her touch was light. He realized the raindrops were not rain, but Kelly's tears.

He heard her voice. "Geeter, stay with me! I need you! I love you. Baby, don't go."

His heart became troubled as his mind drifted. Visions came to him. He was lifting her veil, kissing her beautiful face on their wedding day. He cradled the warmth of their child in his arms. Kelly's body snuggled to him as he held her, dancing slowly under a summer sky with millions of fireflies flittering around them. They sat side by side on the porch watching the sunset, holding hands in rocking chairs. Together they walked through their fields, floating amid the scent of growing corn and the coolness of a spring rain. Her beautiful face appeared before him as they kissed. Geeter tasted her sweet lips on his.

He touched his lips but she wasn't there. Suddenly, her scent filled his lungs. His heart went out to her and the heartbreak she was experiencing. Turning toward his parents, they were now far away. The light from the door was still shining but was less brilliant.

From somewhere deep inside the house, the most wonderful voice said, "The choice is yours, Gideon. If you go back, you can't return for a long time. Your path will be long, hard, and painful. It is your decision, but you must decide now."

Geeter shifted his gaze back to Kelly's tear-stained face. Blood, his blood, was splattered on her cheeks as she tried so desperately to save his life. He turned toward the light, but the glow was rapidly retreating. He again sought Kelly before making his decision.

Horrible pain filled his body. He lurched, grabbing her arms as his eyes met hers.

She screamed in horror at his unexpected movement. Geeter was cold, so cold, except where Kelly was touching him. He tried to tell Kelly something, but the world faded to black.

Chapter 41

K aitlin's back cramped as she held Jeremy's head on her lap. Relief flowed through her limbs when the ambulances arrived. Kelly and K.J. left with Geeter in the first one. Kaitlin held Jeremy's hand as they loaded him in the second unit. Both emergency vehicles roared down the streets to Chicago General with their sirens screaming. The third ambulance was in no hurry and headed to the county morgue.

Arriving at the emergency room, the sisters tried to follow the men, but the staff wouldn't allow it. All they could do was hold and comfort each other. The police finally arrived, and took their statements in a corner of the waiting room. After they were finished, Martina and Nora were there to comfort the two grieving sisters. After K.J. was checked out, Stan took him to Martina's home.

Kaitlin jumped when a nurse called out, "Mrs. Roberts? Is Mrs. Roberts here?"

Kaitlin forced herself to stand. "Here. I'm here."

The nurse motioned for her to follow. "Your husband's in recovery. Want to see him?"

She wrapped her arms around herself in an effort to stem the shaking. All she could manage was a nod before following the nurse behind the closed door. She sat on a stiff, plastic chair. The stainless-steel bed railings were shiny and cold. Jeremy's hair was askew. She lightly ran her fingers through it.

He was unconscious, wrapped in a light chest bandage to hold in the heavier dressings. She squeezed his hand. Her mind drifted back to an earlier time, when Jeremy was in a hospital bed. When it appeared his life was over. And hers, too. The memories were too much.

"Jeremy, I need you. Please. Baby, please..." Her words were slow and erratic. The thought of life without him was devastating.

A soft touch on her shoulder interrupted her concentration. "Are you all right, Mrs. Roberts?"

Kaitlin nodded as she dabbed a tissue at her eyes and turned to the dark-haired woman gazing down on her with an understanding face.

"I'm Doctor Jacobs. I worked on your husband."

"How, how, will he be..." Kaitlin was having trouble getting the words lined up.

The doctor smiled. "He'll be fine. He'll require therapy, but I don't foresee any permanent physically limiting damage." She shook Kaitlin's hand and left.

Kaitlin kept vigil, visions from the previous nightmare haunting her mind. *Open your eyes, sweetheart. I'm waiting. Don't leave me here alone.*

It was early evening when he started to come out of the fog of the anesthesia. Kaitlin again squeezed his hand tightly, softly telling him she loved him. His eyes roved around the room until they found hers.

"How are you, baby?" she asked.

He seemed to be experiencing a lot of pain but tried to hide it. She knew better.

"Better now that I s-see your face. S-so beautiful!"

His words may have been slurred, but there was no sound more wonderful. She smiled and kissed his fingertips. *Just like Jeremy.* The first thing he thought of was her.

He coughed slightly, holding his chest, and stared at her in confusion. "How'd I get here?"

"You were hurt. Remember?"

Jeremy's eyes met hers, but appeared to be trying to look past some sort of filter. "A little fuzzy on what happened." His eyes focused. "Ballister. He shot me."

The crow's feet around his eyes were prominent. *We lived through a lot in two short years.* Kaitlin fought the tears as she clasped and kissed his hand. "He shot you twice, in the chest. The doctor swore you'll be fine."

"Good." Jeremy kept blinking his eyes as he studied her face. "Something's wrong. What is it? You okay?"

Try as she might, she couldn't stop the shaking. "I-I'm okay, I guess."

Jeremy's face turned pale. "He hurt you?"

"No, but I think I'm in shock."

"I understand that. What happened after he shot me?"

She bit her lips to steady herself. "After he shot you, Ballister shot Geeter in the chest. Three times."

Jeremy's face lost all color. His lips trembled. His hands shook. "How is he? He's not dead, is he?"

She leaned forward to kiss his head, loving the warmth of his skin beneath her lips. "I don't think so. Last I knew, he was still in the operating room. The police thought he was dead, but Kelly did CPR on him for a long time to bring him back."

Jeremy's expression changed to one of puzzlement. "If he shot me and Geeter, what happened to Ballister? Did he run away, or did the police get him?"

Here it comes. Her chin started to quiver. She could only shake her head.

Jeremy reached out to comfort her but groaned at the effort. "What happened?"

"Geeter tried to take his gun away."

"And did he?"

"No. Ballister shot Geeter. Kelly was next. He wanted to shoot my sister in the belly to kill her baby."

"Oh God, he didn't, did he?" Jeremy's eyes widened and he stared at her.

She breathed slowly to maintain her composure. "He didn't get the chance." She looked down and her shoulders slumped forward.

He squeezed her hand. "What happened?"

"He died."

"The police shoot him?"

Kaitlin buried her head in her hands. "No. He died from a blow to the head."

"What? Someone hit him? Who?"

The room was slowly turning. She grabbed the bed rail to steady herself. Her voice was a harsh whisper. "I did. I killed him."

His eyes widened as he searched her face. "I don't understand."

"He was going to kill us. I thought you were dead. I needed to protect our girls. As you fell, I grabbed Cassandra's heavy vase. I beat it against his head until it broke. That didn't do it. He grabbed me, then he started shaking. He fell over, dead. I killed him. I'm a murderer. What am I gonna do?"

He squeezed her hand harder. Kaitlin searched his eyes.

"How... how can I live with myself?" The words were difficult to get out.

"You did what you had to do to save our girls. So brave. What else could you do?"

"Nothing. When he pointed the gun at Kelly's belly and said it was time to take care of her bastard child, I had no other option. I grabbed the only weapon I could find. I feel horrible! One minute he was breathing, and the next he was gone. I, uh, I..."

"You did the right thing. You saved Kelly."

The pain oozed down over her, as if someone had thrown a bucket of misery on her head. "Will God ever forgive me?"

He squeezed her hand. "Remember long ago when we were driving and I told you there were no coincidences?"

"Um huh."

"If you hadn't been there, he would have killed Kelly, wouldn't he?"

"Yes, her and her baby."

"Then there was a reason for you to be there. All part of God's plan," Jeremy said softly.

God's plan? "God intended for me to kill my ex-brother-in-law?"

"No. God intended for you to be there to save your sister. You weren't there to take a life, but rather, to save lives. Kelly's, yours, and our children's. God knew this would happen. What would have happened if you didn't?"

"But I could have hit him in the arm or something, you know?"

"And if you did, he probably would have shot you. Katie, listen to me! The man was crazy. You did what you had to do. It was the right thing. God intended for you to be there."

Kaitlin started to say something else, but the nurses were bringing in another patient. Kaitlin turned her head. She recognized the man on the gurney.

Geeter was alive!

Chapter 42

G eeter was in and out of consciousness for the next two days. Either Kelly was there every time he woke up, or he was dreaming about her. His periods of awareness were brief and full of pain, but her presence was his comfort. He finally woke to find his sister Sarah holding his hand, her eyes tired and red.

"Missed you so much," Sarah said. "How ya feelin'?"

The world was fuzzy. *I feel like crap.* "You 'member when we were kids and Dad's mule broke my ribs?"

"Yeah."

"This is worse."

A familiar scent tickled his nostrils. She'd been here. "How's Kelly?"

"She's doing fine. We changed places a few minutes ago. Been at your side most of the time since you were shot. Saved your life, she did."

A mixture of sensations hit him. Joy, pain, loss, relief, love. Sarah's face wavered as his mind's eye went back to the incident. "I remember. Mom and Daddy were there."

Her expression was one of shock. "Couldn't be. They're dead, Geeter."

"I know. But they were there. Aunt Lilly and Grandpa, too. And so many others who's gone on. All there, right on the porch. And there was this beautiful light coming out of the door. I think it was Jesus."

Sarah stared at him in astonishment. "I-I-I don't understand."

"I was going toward the light. Then Kelly touched me. Her tears fell on my face. Sarah, my life... no, my future flashed before my eyes. And this voice, this beautiful voice came out of the light telling me to choose. I came back. Kelly needed me."

A sudden sob came from the doorway.

Geeter's mouth dropped open. "Becky."

She nodded slightly. "Geeter."

"Didn't know you were here."

"I know. Sarah and me flew up when we heard what happened. The three of us been sittin' with you round the clock."

"Three?"

"Yeah. Sarah and me. And her... *Kelly*."

Sarah softly touched his hand. His shoulders trembled as he watched Becky's face. Sarah kissed her brother's forehead and quietly left the room.

"Becky, so glad to see you."

"Good to see you awake, Geeter. I-I can't stay..."

"Sit and talk to me, Becky."

She shook her head. "No."

His chest tightened when a stray teardrop dribbled down her cheek. "What's wrong?"

"Just the emotion of seeing you awake. They said you might not pull through, but you did. I'm so glad."

"Me, too."

Becky squeezed his hand. "Gonna say goodbye now."

"Goodbye?" he questioned. He was confused and not just from the pain medication. "Why you saying goodbye?"

She wiped her cheeks. "I need to go. Just wanted to know you're going to be all right, that's all."

"But I don't understand. Why are you leavin'?"

Becky paused for a few seconds, perhaps to calm down. "When I got here, Kelly was sitting with you. My heart got all tangled up inside."

"I don't understand."

"The look on her face. If I never see love again, I saw it as she sat with you." She turned toward the door. "I've got to go, now."

"Wait. Don't go. I... I love you, Becky."

Her smile was bittersweet. "And I love you, Geeter, and I always will. But you love Kelly much more than you'll ever love me. That's plain to see. I won't stand in your way. That's why I'm leaving."

"Yeah, I love her, but not like I love you!" He was so tired.

"I know, but I lost one husband because he took another woman. I won't compete with Kelly. Refuse to go through that again. I can't and I won't."

"But Becky, this ain't fair! I'm stuck in this bed, just waking up. Don't do this to me. I love you much more than you know!"

She smiled at him through her tears. "I know, but would you take a bullet for me like you did for Kelly?" She watched his reaction, his eyes. "If you and Kelly were together, would you drop everything and run to my side?"

His eyelids were so heavy. "But you told me to go to her, Becky!"

"I did, but I prayed inside you wouldn't. But you did. And Kelly loves you, Geeter. I had hoped when I got here, it'd be different. But by the look on her face as she sat next to you in this bed, there's no doubt she's in love with you. And besides, she's carrying a child that might be yours."

"But it might not be."

"Will it really matter? Be honest."

Geeter looked away from her. He sighed. "No, Becky. It won't. I'll always consider that child mine."

"You still love her, don't you?"

Geeter's mind was foggy. His eyelids were drooping. "I don't know. I did, very much. But then things happened. Don't know what I feel right now."

"I do. I can read you."

Both of them were quiet for a moment, and Geeter couldn't help it. He fell asleep.

***

She watched him sleep. Moving close to the bed, Becky held his hand for a brief moment. She brushed his hair from his eyes before softly kissing his brow, then his lips. She whispered, "Goodbye, my love."

Becky walked out to find Kelly waiting in the hallway. With tears in her eyes, she turned to Kelly. "He's all yours. Please take care of him for me." Becky turned, walked down the hallway, and out of their lives, forever.

***

Kelly sat by Geeter's side, holding his hand. The buzz of the hospital was faint in her ears, but his breathing was loud, what she focused on. It seemed to be days before he started to move. She waited, not knowing what he would say.

His eyes found hers. "Kelly. How are you?"

"Fine, but the real question is, how are you?"

He moved his head from side to side. "Well..."

Need to get this over with. Kelly cleared her throat. "I know Becky was here to see you. What did she say?"

His eyes wrinkled. From confusion or disbelief? "She said... goodbye."

"How'd that make you feel?"

"Confused. Not sure why. You know why she left?"

"Not really, but I think it was because of me." Her chest tightened, arms tingled. "Are you sad about that?"

He studied her eyes before responding. "Yes, no, maybe. I loved her, Kelly. Thought she loved me too, but she left. I'm so confused."

Kelly blushed. "She did love you. Maybe that's why she left."

His face screwed up as he gazed at her. "Still don't understand. If she loved me, why'd she go?"

This was the make-or-break moment. Kelly's heart was in her throat. "She left because she knew I'm in love with you, too. I realized it right after I told you I just wanted to be friends." Her eyes were suddenly scratchy. "I regretted saying that as soon as it left my lips. I hurt you that day. My life was in shambles. I was confused, upset. I hope you can forgive me. Do you still love me, somewhere down deep inside?"

He stared at her for the longest time, alternating his gaze between her eyes and her lips. He nodded. "I do, but can we start again?"

Her feet were light. Even the harsh glow from the overhead lights was beautiful. She felt her whole face smile. "Yes, we can, but don't be surprised if we go a lot faster this time." Kelly kissed his hand. "By the way, I wanted to thank you for saving me."

"Heard you saved me, too. Thank you. Besides, I think you'da done the same for me, roles reversed and everything."

I'd like to think I would have. Her heart swelled. "I doubt that, but you, you're a true hero."

They smiled, holding hands for a while. Hurdle number one cleared, now for number two. "We need to talk about your condition. You remember the doctor being here?"

His eyes rolled out of focus. "Maybe, but everything's a little fuzzy."

"It's okay. The doctor gave you good and bad news. You told the doctor you have feeling in your feet, but he said you can't move your legs. Can you?"

Geeter's eyes focused on his legs. The veins in his temples bulged, but nothing happened. He shook his head and sadly said, "No, I can't. Am I paralyzed?"

Tears started to form in her eyes. She brushed them away. "Maybe, you see, they couldn't remove one of the bullets. It's nestled against your spinal column. You'll need additional surgery to remove it, but there's a risk and no guarantee. The doctor said you have a 50-50 chance of getting movement back. He wants to wait until you're stronger."

Geeter nodded as he studied her face. "What happened after Ballister shot me?"

She shuddered as she recalled the horror of that day. "He was going to kill me and the baby. Katie came to my rescue. She killed Ballister."

He nodded. "That's what I thought. It was really strange." He told her about his near-death experience. After he finished, he stared at the wall, avoiding eye contact.

She could read his mind. *It's okay. It won't matter.* "Geeter, listen to me. Even if you don't get movement back in your legs, I'll be here with you. I'll never leave you... that is, unless you don't want me here."

He still didn't look her in the eyes. "I do want you here. It's just that I'd only be half a man."

Anger built in her. *Don't you dare!* "Like hell. You're more of a man than anyone I've ever known."

He looked out the window. "Yeah, right. A cripple. What could I possible offer to you in life? There's no way you'd ever want me."

She kissed his hand. "You're wrong. You see, I've had a lot of time to think about what I really want in life. It comes down to one thing."

"What's that?"

She smiled. "Sure you want to know?"

"Yeah, 'course I do."

"I'm going out on a limb here. Don't let me fall off."

His face sported both confusion and concern. "I won't. I'm your friend, and you can tell me anything, anything at all."

Her heart fluttered. "Okay, remember that. The thing I want more than anything in life is not a thing. It's a person. And that person is you, Geeter. I want to spend my life with you."

His mouth dropped in shock.

"Do you want to spend your life with me, too?"

"I-I-I don't know. Not too long ago, I felt that way about you, but... What happens if you change your mind? Things changed. I'm no longer a real man."

Kelly put her finger to his lips. "Stop saying that. I love you."

He hesitated. "I-I-I love you, too, but what happened to starting over?"

She blushed. "We did say that, didn't we? Look, for too long I held my true feelings from you." The look in his eyes told her she was pushing too fast, too hard. "I know I hurt you. I'm not expecting you to feel like this right now, but if there is ever even the slightest chance... I don't ever want to keep anything from you, whether we just become very good friends or something more."

Geeter stared at his legs. The next words he said were lies, and she knew it. "Kelly, I don't know how I feel."

I can't begin to understand what you're going through. "That's fair. Let's just put that aside for now." Kelly's heart rate was slowing down, back to double digits. *Please let the seeds of love I planted bear good fruit.* "Let's concentrate on getting you better."

Their conversation was tiring him. "You just rest for a while. Your sister wants to come back in." She kissed his forehead and turned to go. She squeezed his hand before she moved toward the door.

"Kelly?"

She looked over a shoulder back at him. "Yes?"

"Thank you. Let's just take it slow for a while. I don't know how I feel. I'm sorry. I'm real confused."

She smiled. *Liar. Your eyes gave you away.* "It's all right. If God intends us to be, we will. If not, it won't happen. But if it does, I promise you I will love you and be by your side forever."

He looked like he was in pain. "Kelly..."

Her voice was barely a whisper. "No matter what happens, Geeter, I'm in love with you and time will never change that." She let go of his hand and left.

Sarah was waiting in the hallway. Kelly wrapped her arms around her for a long while. Kelly didn't move away from the door when Sarah entered. Instead, she listened to the conversation. Geeter and Sarah discussed his condition, and the risks and potential gains of the surgery to remove the bullet nestling against his spine. Together, they decided that the potential benefits outweighed the risks. Geeter asked Sarah to speak with the doctor. Kelly sent another prayer to heaven.

Chapter 43

G eeter's operation was scheduled for the same day Jeremy was to be released. Kelly waited while Kaitlin took Jeremy home, turning his care over to Nora and Stan. She was glad her sister would return to be with her while they operated on Geeter. Sarah couldn't stay. She had to return to Tennessee.

Gratitude filled Kelly when Kaitlin walked in. Kelly held her so tightly she could feel Kaitlin's heartbeat. She needed to set something straight. "Katie, I want to apologize again. I'm so sorry for what I put you two through."

Her little sister cupped her face to look into her eyes. Kaitlin smiled at her. "No clue what you're talking about. Something happened, but I put it out of my mind, for good. I came here to sit with my best friend while she waits."

Kelly hugged her sister again, basking in forgiveness. She'd expected Kaitlin would never talk to her again. All the stress she'd suffered turned her into something she wasn't, but Kaitlin had forgiven her. She whispered in her sister's ear, "Why did you forgive me?"

"Why? Because you mean so much to me. I have so many good memories that involve you. I love you. Now, let's never talk about the bad times, again. Okay?"

Kelly squeezed Kaitlin's hands and kissed her cheek.

"Now, I came here to be with you while we wait for Geeter to get out of surgery. Let's talk about the good times between you two, okay? And not a word about the kidnapping or anything bad that followed."

Kelly was thirsty. She took a drink from a water bottle. Warm, but still wet. "Still can't believe the man I married could do that."

"It wasn't him. You know that. When they did the autopsy, they found the brain tumor. Remember the psychiatrist saying that the tumor affected his thinking?"

"Yes. Thank you for saving my life. You were a superhero, killing him with that vase. You never liked it anyway."

Kaitlin stiffened and coldly replied, "I didn't kill him. The aneurism caused by the tumor killed him."

The hurt was evident in Kaitlin's eyes. Kelly backpedaled, "I didn't mean to..."

"Don't talk about that anymore. Let's focus on Geeter. You have to believe he will get better. I know he will."

Kelly shivered despite the warmth of the room. *Geeter's biggest fear*. "Suppose he can't walk again? Can you imagine how horrible that'll be for him?"

Kaitlin frowned. "It'll be different, but not horrible. Will it make a difference to you?"

Kelly shook her head. "Not to me, but it'll be tough for him. He loves that farm. I told you what he said about it after he was shot."

"Do you mean when he saw his parents and heard Jesus's voice?"

"Yes. Heaven to him was that farm." Her eyes teared again because she was the reason it happened. *Please God*. Kaitlin's hand was warm where it touched her arm.

"I also remember he said he had a decision to make about whether to come back or not, right?"

"He did, Katie."

"And he came back. Because he loved you. Because you needed him."

"I hope so. I feel so bad he got shot, protecting me."

Kaitlin touched her cheek. "Kelly, one thing Jeremy taught me, and I really believe this, is there's a purpose for everything. God has a plan. That's why those two bullets didn't take Jeremy's life. God has something awesome planned for Jeremy, a purpose he hasn't yet filled. Maybe to raise our daughters, I don't know."

The love and zeal her younger sister had was so real. Kelly could almost see it, almost touch it. "Maybe he hasn't spoiled you enough yet!"

"Jeremy doesn't spoil me!" Kaitlin snapped.

Kelly's laughter built. "Liar." They both laughed. "You don't know how lucky you are!"

"Yes, yes, I do! I'm the luckiest woman on earth, but we're missing the point. The point is, Geeter isn't done, either. He has something yet to do. And Kelly, I really believe what he has to do revolves around you."

Kelly's face heated. "I hope so."

"You really love him, don't you?"

The desire in her heart was making her dizzy. "Um-huh. More than anything."

"Only because he saved you?"

Kelly didn't even have to think about it. "Not at all! I love him because he's wonderful. So gentle and kind. He's always treated me like I'm something special, like a precious jewel. And he loves me as I am, damaged and all. Never controlling. He talks to me, asks my opinion and supports me. I never had that before. And to think... I t-told him I only w-wanted to be friends." Kelly choked up.

Kaitlin lightly smacked her hand. "Stop it. Look at the two of us. A bundle of emotions, all fueled by hormones."

"And drama."

Kaitlin smiled. "And drama. Does he love you?"

Kelly hesitated. "I'm pretty sure he does, but he's holding back from admitting it. Because he doesn't think he's a man."

"What?"

"Because he can't walk. I thought I had it good with Ballister, but what Geeter and I share is so much better."

Kaitlin smiled. "I think so, too."

A light suddenly came on inside. "Maybe you're right that everything happens for a reason. I think the best thing Ballister ever did was to divorce me. He was so controlling and self-centered, it was pathetic."

Kaitlin stared at her. "Everyone in the family thought you two were happy!"

Kelly slowly nodded. "I did, too. But there were so many things you didn't see or know. So controlling, so obsessive."

Kaitlin changed position as she sat. "I never knew."

"Never told you this. I made the mistake of telling Ballister how wonderful I thought Jeremy was after you two got engaged. He became so jealous, so obsessed with the thought of you two. He would... No, I'm not going to tell you, but it was wrong. He was so jealous of Jeremy and what he had—you." Kelly stopped for a second before continuing softly. "I was afraid if I told you, you'd be upset with me."

Kaitlin shook her head. "Never, but maybe that's why he hated Jeremy so much. That must have been rough on you. And I didn't see it."

"I was naïve. Then when my world was falling apart, you were so happy. I couldn't stand it. I think that's why I said those horrible things to you."

Kaitlin shook her head. "Kelly, we aren't going there. What's past is past. Okay?"

"I had to explain it. Jeremy never did anything with me. Didn't even flirt with me. You're so lucky to have someone who treats you so sweetly and is obviously so in love with you. I really envy you, sis."

"Thanks for sharing with me, Kelly, but let's let sleeping dogs lie. Now, tell me about being with Geeter." They talked for hours until a nurse came in and told them Geeter was in recovery.

The nurses weren't as strict at this hospital, so both Kaitlin and Kelly were allowed to be at Geeter's side. He was in recovery for about half an hour before the effects of the anesthesia started to wear off. Kelly made sure the first face he saw was hers. His sleepy smile was a happy one, and he reached for her hand. Kaitlin stayed only long enough to say hello, then gave him a quick kiss on the cheek and left.

Kelly didn't say much but sat next to him, spoon-feeding him ice chips.

Before long, the surgeon came in. "Hello, Gideon! How are you?"

Geeter appeared to be well medicated and probably didn't feel much, yet. "I think I'm fine, Doc. But you tell me, how am I?"

"The surgery went well. I was able to remove the bullet, but your nerves were swollen and bruised. I'm cautiously optimistic. Hopefully when the swelling goes down, you'll regain control of your muscles. But we'll have to wait and see. We'll keep you here for three or four days, then discharge you. Will you be staying in this area, or will you go back to Tennessee?"

Not losing you again. Before Geeter could reply, Kelly answered, "He'll be staying with me here in Chicago. I already ordered a hospital bed for him." She kissed his head, allowing her cheek to rest against his forehead. So warm, so alive. "We'll all be staying with Kaitlin and Jeremy."

Geeter shook his head. "Nope. If I'm here, you'll have to take care of me. Maybe I should go to a rehab hospital.

I mean, I can't even get up to go to the bathroom. I don't want you to have to wipe my butt every time I need to go."

Kelly laughed. "Are you that confused that you don't remember what I did for a living?" She touched the end of his nose. "And besides, I want to be the one who takes care of you, unless you really don't want me to." She hoped her smile convinced him.

"But what about your job?"

"Oh, forgot to tell you. My ex-husband never got around to changing his will. He was insured to the max. I won't ever have to work again, unless I want to."

Geeter's mouth dropped open. The physician laughed. "You might want to take her up on that. Not many men get to have such a pretty and loving nurse. My office will contact you after your discharge. I'll want to see you next Monday. Don't push things, just rest, and I think we will see good results. Good luck. See you next week." He shook both of their hands and left.

Chapter 44

G eeter was happier, yet sadder than ever. As promised, Kelly cared for him. Kaitlin's happy home became filled once again as Jeremy and Geeter rehabilitated together.

He smiled. Rarely in recorded history had two patients been as spoiled as they were. They had not only Kaitlin and Kelly to care for them, but also Nora and Stan and Kelly's four children.

The warmth of the sun shining through the big windows relaxed him. He and Kelly had grown so close. They didn't talk about whether they were in love or not, but Geeter knew the truth. His heart almost beat out of his chest every time he saw her. But there was one big problem. He couldn't walk. Wasn't whole. He'd never be the man she needed, unless things changed. If they didn't soon, he'd have to leave her. For her sake.

Kelly waited on him hand and foot, her scent enticing him. They read books and played games together. In the evenings, Kelly's children joined in. Sometimes, the closeness brought tears to his eyes. This was something he never dreamed he would have. This was how a family should be, the one he wanted.

One afternoon, the delectable aroma of homemade apple cobbler filled the room. Stan came in , followed by Nora carrying a tray of bowls with cobbler and vanilla ice cream on top. "I made something special for my favorite hero."

Melting ice cream mingled with spiced apple. "Ma'am, this is really great. Good thing I don't live here all the time. If I did, I'd weigh as much as an old Angus bull."

"Glad you like it. And please, call me Mom, not ma'am."

Her fondness brought a warmth to his chest. Love. Kindness. Acceptance.

Stan finished and placed his empty bowl back on the tray. The way he looked at Geeter told him something important was coming. "So when you get better, what's the first thing you're going to do?"

Geeter didn't hesitate. "I'll sweep your daughter into my arms, tell her how much I love her, and beg her to marry me... uh... with your permission, of course."

Stan chuckled. "Which you'll have. And if you can't walk again?"

There it was. The bane of his worries. "Then I'll let her find happiness with a man who can walk straight and tall. Someone who'll make her happy. A *real* man." Despite the wonderful taste of the cobbler, it was sticking in his craw.

Stan patted his shoulder. "Nonsense. Son, you're a real man, regardless if you never take another step again. As far as making my daughter happy, you already have."

***

By late April, Jeremy had recovered enough to return to work on a limited basis. Geeter's progress was slower. While he had full feeling in his legs and at times could will them to move a little bit, the control of his leg movement was spastic and unpredictable. Despite the slow gains of rehabilitation, he remained positive and upbeat. His surgeon recommended an aggressive physical therapy.

He was referred to the Chicago Center for Sports Medicine, where Jeremy had rehabilitated after being injured in a vehicle accident. Geeter started there on a five-day-a-week schedule. They had a children's area in the building. Kelly often brought David along, because his other siblings were in school. Quite often, she'd grab lunch, and the two or three of them would have a picnic in the inside gardens. One Friday, Kelly became so engrossed in the time they spent together that she forgot about her obstetrician appointment.

***

One day in mid-May, the rehab clinic was closed due to a water main break. Stan and Nora were off visiting friends while Geeter and Kelly played Scrabble. She loved the feel of the wooden tiles and the colors on the board. Just like her sister Kaitlin, Kelly played at the expert level. To her surprise, Geeter was giving her a run for her money. She was searching for a double-word spot to take the lead when the doorbell rang.

Kelly pointed her finger at Geeter. "Don't peek at my tiles. I'll be right back." She lifted Davy off the floor and handed him to Geeter.

The scent of tulips from the yard greeted her as she opened the door. Her temperature shot through the roof. *Todd.* Without a word, he walked inside, uninvited.

"What are you doing here?" Kelly demanded.

"I'm here to see you and my baby. Tell me why you missed last week's obstetrician appointment."

Jerk! Like I need to tell you anything. His controlling attitude raised the temperature of her anger a few more degrees. "I don't have to explain a damn thing to you. And who do you think you are, barging into my home and interrogating me?"

He stuck his face in hers, and the smell of stale coffee sickened her. "I'm the father of our child, and even though the baby is in your womb, it's half mine! Why did you miss that appointment?"

Kelly turned to go, but Todd grabbed her, and twisted her arm so she had to face him. The pain was intense. "Let go! You're hurting me!"

He squeezed her arm tighter. "You'll learn to answer me when I ask you a question."

"Let go!"

He grabbed her hair, yanking hard. "You owe me an answer. I won't leave without one. That baby deserves decent care, and I don't care if I have to drag you there. We are going to the doctor right now!"

Kelly kicked him in the shin as hard as she could, to no avail. "Let go of me."

Todd increased the pressure on her arm, forcing her to her knees. "Want to play rough? Two can play at that game."

He yanked her arm unmercifully. Kelly squeezed her eyes shut as the pain increased. Suddenly, he let go.

Kelly gasped when she opened her eyes! Geeter had his right hand wrapped around Todd's throat.

Geeter growled, "Don't you ever lay a hand on her again. You do, you better be prepared to meet your maker." He roughly shoved him toward the door. "Now, git outta my sight and never come back, ya hear?"

Todd pulled himself up, steadying himself on the door frame. His eyes flitted back and forth between Kelly and Geeter. Geeter slowly shuffled toward him. "You hard of hearing, boy? I said git!" Geeter reached toward Todd, but before he could touch him, the doctor ran down the porch steps.

Geeter closed the door and turned to Kelly. "You okay? Did he hurt you?"

Her breath refused to come out. She was in shock. Davy tugged on the leg of her jeans and reached for her. She scooped him up, then turned to stare at Geeter.

His eyes clouded. "Kelly, answer me, please. You okay?" He took a feeble step toward her.

Kelly was having trouble seeing. "G-G-Geeter, look what happened!"

"I'm sorry. I should have answered the door. Are you okay?"

"I can't... is what I'm seeing... Geeter, look at you!"

"What about me? Are you upset I kicked him out?"

She couldn't believe her eyes. The words formed in her mind but wouldn't come out of her mouth.

David said it for her. He pointed at Geeter. "Look, Mommy. Geeter can walk."

Kelly nodded in disbelief. "I know, Davy, I know! Geeter, you're walking. It's a miracle!"

Geeter suddenly realized he was on his feet. He stretched his arms to steady himself. He had moisture in his eyes as he reached for Kelly. "Honey, come here!"

Kelly set David down and gingerly slipped into Geeter's arms. His kiss was gentle. He whispered for the first time in a long time, "I love you, Kelly!"

He pulled away, holding her as his eyes searched hers. "Kelly, now that I can walk again, I need to ask you something." His brown eyes shimmered as if tons of glitter were released in them.

"What's that?"

Geeter grinned. "Kelly, will you marry me?"

Winning the Super Bowl, World Series, and the lottery all at the same time couldn't compare to the joy in her heart. She kissed him, whispering in his ear, "Yes, yes, yes!"

Chapter 45

S itting in the backyard, Kelly absorbed the warmth of the sun as the scent of fresh cut grass surrounded her. The first months of their marriage passed in total bliss. She grew larger, and the obstetrician remarked how strong the heartbeat was from the life inside her womb. Geeter and Kelly were living their future. Geeter had legally adopted her four children, so now they were all Smiths.

The baby moved delicately inside her womb. "Soon as you're born, little one, we're moving to Tennessee." Seeing the excitement in her husband's eyes as he described the farm, she fell in love with the idea of raising their children in the country. Geeter had offered to sell the farm so they could stay in Chicago, close to Kelly's family. Even though Kelly was moved by that, she knew what the farm meant to him. They decided to build another house on the property. Everything was just perfect in Kelly's life, well almost.

She had lost sleep worrying about her sister. While Kelly's pregnancy had been easy, Kaitlin was having a rough time. Her slight build was not used to the extra weight of the twins, and her back bothered her constantly. She'd contracted gestational diabetes and in her eighth month, her physician put her on total bed rest.

As a nurse, Kelly knew those symptoms were routine. But the other symptoms were more troubling.

She remembered the day she'd knocked softly on the white painted door. *"Katie?"*

There was no response. Kelly entered, finding her sister on top of the covers in a fetal position, staring at the wall.

"I'm going to miss you so much," Kaitlin cried.

Kelly assumed she was talking about the move to Tennessee. *"Aw. You know we'll constantly be visiting. It wouldn't matter where we live. You and me, we've got this special bond, and nothing will keep us apart."*

Kaitlin cried harder. *"I won't make it."*

Kelly's spine tingled not so much at the words, but rather at the conviction of them. *"Won't make what?"*

"Through childbirth. For the last week, I've had these terrible dreams. Something goes wrong, and I die before I can hold my babies."

First time mother fears. *"You're wrong. It's just jitters."*

Kaitlin rolled away from her. *"You sound like Jeremy. He doesn't believe me either."*

Kelly's worries grew when Kaitlin confided to her that her recurring nightmares had intensified. Jeremy could no longer kiss them away. Kaitlin's fear grew exponentially. She didn't confide in anyone else.

Because Kaitlin was bearing twins, the obstetrician had scheduled a C-section for the twenty-first of August. Jeremy had to travel the week before the procedure. A chocolate donut hole was tempting Kelly when she heard Kaitlin shout out her name from upstairs.

Kelly raced to Kaitlin's bedroom. "What's up, Katie?"

Kaitlin's face was contorted in pain. "I think I'm having contractions! Can you call Jeremy and tell him I need him to come home, now?"

Kelly dialed the number. "Jeremy, it's Kelly. Any way you can come home? Katie's having contractions."

"They just closed the door on the jet." His voice suddenly became muffled. "Stewardess! I've got a family emergency. I need off this plane, now." The confusion of multiple voices all talking at once in the background were surpassed by Jeremy's raised voice. "I know we haven't pushed off, yet. I need off this plane right now!" Additional conversation was followed by the click of the overhead compartment lock. The voice was louder now and was directed to Kelly. "I only have a carry-on. I'll be off here in five. Can I speak to Katie?"

Kelly started to hand the phone to Kaitlin, but Kaitlin cried out in pain from a severe contraction. "Now's not a good time! I'll call the doctor and keep you updated." Kelly hung up and turned to her sister. Kaitlin was sweating and her face was red. Her eyes were moist as she grasped Kelly's hand. Kelly lost feeling in her fingers from her sister's grip.

"Kel, this is the part where I die."

"You're not going to die," Kelly said and immediately called to Geeter downstairs, "We need to get Katie to the hospital. It's time!"

Geeter raced up and before Kelly could get Kaitlin out of bed, he swept his sister-in-law in his arms and carried her to the car. Then he came back in the door and stooped to kiss the children who were with Stan and Nora in the living room before turning to walk Kelly outside.

Kelly's face had gone pale.

"What's wrong?" Geeter asked.

"I think I'm having contractions, too!"

Geeter yelled, "What?"

"A contraction, maybe. It was only one, but it was very strong." She knelt to kiss the kids.

Nora laughed. "Geeter, you better step on it and get both my daughters to the hospital."

"Should I call the doctor?"

Kelly grabbed his arm. "You drive. I'll call the doctor!"

Geeter drove cautiously fast to the hospital.

Kaitlin blubbered as an aide helped her into a wheelchair at the admissions entrance. "I want to see Jeremy before they take me in to do the C-section. Call him and tell him to hurry, Geeter."

Geeter stepped out.

Kelly understood the pain. Knew how frightening it was the first time.

Kaitlin reached for Kelly. "I need to see him, Kel. Need to tell him how much I love him one last time.

Her sister's conviction scared Kelly to the core. She tried to reassure her. "It was just a bad dream. Everything will be fine."

Geeter returned.

Kaitlin was crying harder. "I want my husband."

Kelly gave her sister a quick hug. Suddenly, wetness ran down Kelly's legs, covering the floor at her feet. *My water broke.*

The aide arranged for a second wheelchair and soon Kelly was moved to a bed next to Kaitlin's so she could hold her sister's hand.

Kaitlin screamed out, "I need pain medication."

A nurse checked her vitals and stated, "Too late, sister. Time to get you to the OR."

The transport team entered and lifted Kaitlin onto the gurney. When Kaitlin turned to look at her, fear shook Kelly. Kelly saw the eyes not of her baby sister, but of a trapped and desperate animal.

"Goodbye, Kelly," Kaitlin whimpered. "P-please help Jeremy with the girls and tell them how much I loved them!"

Kelly had trouble focusing because of fear. She called after her, "I love you, too, Katie. You'll be fine. I'll see you soon, and we can look at our babies together."

***

Jeremy raced in, gasping for air after sprinting from the parking garage. He ran down the corridor. His eyes searched inside the room. Kelly and Geeter were on one side. A second bed was messed up, as if someone had just been there.

Geeter called, "You missed her by less than a minute. They took her to the OR. Out, to the left. Hurry, you'll catch her."

He was worried. Because of her nightmares. They had taunted him the whole way from the airport. He ran down the hallway, stopping when he heard Kaitlin crying. He ran onward and collided with a linen cart when he rounded the corner too fast. He caught sight of her at the last turn before the operating room. "Stop!" he screamed. He reached for and clung to his wife, breathing in her essence.

She cried in his arms, her words almost incoherent. "Hoped you'd make it! I love you. Wanted to tell you one last time. Goodbye,"

"This isn't goodbye. I'll be there holding your hand when you wake up," Jeremy said.

They had the cart moving again. Kaitlin's long, curvy fingers clasping his, refusing to let go. "Love you. Forever."

A nurse pushed Jeremy out of the way. Kaitlin's nightmares terrified him more than anything he'd ever felt. There was no way he could... He dropped to his knees in prayer right there in the maternity ward.

***

This was it, time to deliver. The doctor finished the exam. "All right, Kelly. Next contraction, I want you to push."

Kelly gripped Geeter's hand for support. The next contraction came, and she pushed, screaming out in pain. Geeter was trying to be supportive, but his voice broke as he whispered she was doing a great job and also how much he loved her.

The contraction ended. "Great job, Kelly! The baby is crowning. Another one or two and your child will be here."

The next contraction hit hard, and she pushed with all her might. David's birth had come quickly, but this one was the fastest yet. Her efforts pushed the baby out of the birth canal and into the doctor's hands. "It's a girl, Kelly! Congratulations! Daddy, would you like to cut the umbilical cord?"

Kelly collapsed back onto the bed, laughing, crying, breathing heavily. *Thank you, thank you, thank you!*

Geeter kissed his wife, then smiled at her. The nurse clamped the cord and handed him the surgical scissors. He took his first look at his daughter. He cut the cord then fainted.

Chapter 46

The aching in Jeremy's chest would kill him. His shirt was drenched. He was still on his knees, praying, when the door swung open.

"Mr. Roberts, come quickly! Your wife is giving birth!"

He forced himself to his feet, following her. "What?"

"Before we could get her on the table, her water broke. The doctor decided to let her give birth naturally."

She handed him a gown and mask which he quickly donned. The nurse opened the double doors to the OR, and they entered together. Kaitlin was leaning back against the partially elevated bed.

He ran to her side and held her soft, warm hand. But when he caught sight of her face, his heart almost stopped. Her face was blanched, and she wore a mask of pain. He wasn't even sure she knew he was there.

"Katie, it's me, Jeremy. I'm right here with you."

It was as if she didn't see or hear him. Her eyes were focused on a space on the opposite wall. Suddenly, Kaitlin screamed as the pain of another strong contraction racked her body.

"Keep pushing, Katie!" the doctor said. "Your first daughter is coming."

Kaitlin pushed and her firstborn came into the world and landed in the doctor's hands. Before he could do anything, the baby let out a quiet cry.

Jeremy was so excited and kissed his wife. She didn't seem to notice. She stared blankly as if she weren't aware of anything. Jeremy gazed at the doctor, and his heart gathered in his throat. Jeremy didn't like what he saw in the doctor's eyes. He wasn't sure if it was worry or fear.

Jeremy glanced down at Kaitlin's crotch and saw it. Blood, lots of blood flowing heavily onto the table. His stomach turned.

The doctor motioned to the nurse. "Get him out of here. Page the rapid response team and tell them we need the mass transfusion protocol."

Alarms screamed on the monitors. Jeremy stared at the blinking numbers. One of the nurses said, "Heartbeat on the second baby is falling rapidly."

Jeremy glanced at Kaitlin. Her eyes were on him. In all the confusion, her voice seemed to come from somewhere else. "Please remember me and don't forget... that..." Katie's head dropped against her shoulder.

The anesthesiologist's voice was high as he yelled, "I need to intubate her. Get Mr. Roberts out of here, now."

"This can't be happening. Where the hell is that rapid response team? Page them again, stat!"

The nurse's grip was firm as she pushed him from the room. The doors closed, separating Jeremy from everything he cared about in the world.

***

The irritating smell of ammonia brought Geeter back to consciousness. He sat on the floor until the fuzziness left and he re-oriented himself. The nurse helped him to his feet after checking his blood pressure.

"Geeter, come hold our little girl," Kelly called softly.

He kissed his wife, then reached for his baby girl. The blanket was softer than rabbit fur, his daughter lighter than a feather. He was afraid to touch her, afraid he would break her.

Kelly giggled at him. "Honey, she's not fine china! Hold her tight and give your baby girl a kiss."

Geeter held her, his little girl, dancing around the room before returning and giving Kelly a long and gentle kiss. "I love you, Kelly!"

Her smile was radiant. In fact, his beautiful wife glowed. "Love you, too, Daddy."

Geeter had never known such joy, the joy of being a daddy. When it was time for Kelly to nurse, Geeter excused himself. There were so many people he had to call. But as he walked toward the elevator, he passed the chapel. A man was sitting in the front pew, staring at the cross. The man's back was facing Geeter, but Geeter recognized him. It was none other than the man who had bravely saved his life in Iraq. The man who was his best friend. It was Jeremy.

Geeter didn't understand. He walked up to him. Jeremy was slowly turning his wedding ring between his fingers. Something wasn't right. Jeremy didn't seem to notice he was there.

"You okay, L.T.?"

Jeremy's gaze didn't leave the cross. "It lasts forever, you know? Just goes on and on. Like this ring. Once it starts, it has no end."

"What are you talkin' about?"

"Love. It's the only thing that matters."

"Something bad happen?"

Jeremy nodded his head. "Um-hmm."

"The babies okay?"

Jeremy shrugged his shoulders. "Wouldn't know."

"Katie all right?"

Jeremy sobbed and wiped his eyes with his sleeve. He didn't answer, but shook his head.

Geeter touched his arm. "Why don't you come with me? We'll go see Kelly."

Jeremy hung his head. He inserted his finger back in his wedding ring. "Okay."

***

Kelly snuggled with her little girl. She counted toes and fingers. The baby's hair was blonde. *Just like mommy's.* Kelly glanced up when the door opened. A cold chill ran up her spine when Jeremy entered, his stare blank as he shuffled his feet.

"What's wrong?" Kelly asked softly.

As if in slow motion, Jeremy's head turned toward her, but stopped when he saw the baby.

"Jeremy?" Kelly said.

Jeremy's stare was vacant. "She's perfect, you know?"

She couldn't shake the eerie feeling. Something wasn't right. "Want to see her?"

"Such a unique blend of beauty, kindness, and grace. Wonderful sense of humor, so kind, so loving. I was the luckiest man in the world to win her heart."

Kelly shared a worried look with Geeter.

"Kelly, I never asked you for anything, did I?"

She shook her head. "No, you never did."

"Adopt our girls."

Oh no. God, please no. "Why would you even say anything like that?"

His face screwed up. "Lost my mom when I was thirteen. Those girls will need a mom, a home filled with love." He stopped and wiped his eyes with the palm of his hands.

"Where's Katie? Jeremy, how's my sister?"

243

He raised his eyes to finally meet hers. Their color was no longer electric blue, but now a paler color.

Kelly's chin quivered. She whispered, "Katie?"

Jeremy sniffed hard. "Katie's gone. Her nightmares came true."

Kelly screamed, "No, no, no!" Kelly turned to Geeter in horror. "She can't be gone. You must be wrong."

Jeremy's chest heaved. "The doctor said they were losing her. They chased me out. More than two hours ago. My wonderful wife is... is dead."

Kelly stared in disbelief, too horrified to move.

Jeremy cleared his throat. His expression was scary. "It's time," he said. "Take care, Kelly."

What? "Where are you going?"

"To be with my wife. I'm not strong enough to live another moment without her."

"Jeremy, no, please," Kelly begged.

Like lightning, Geeter moved to block Jeremy from the door.

As if for the first time, Jeremy looked at Geeter. "Bye, my friend."

"Stop it, Jeremy."

Jeremy stared at Geeter. "First time you ever called me Jeremy."

"You're my brother, Jeremy."

"Move, Geeter."

"No."

"Get out of my way. If you don't, I'll hurt you. I can take you any day."

"Yep. Any other day. But not today. You saved my life in Iraq. I'm savin' yours. Let us get you some help."

Kelly knew it was coming. Jeremy's fists balled. Geeter moved his right foot back to brace himself.

A knock on the door interrupted all three of them.

***

A very tired looking man stood in the doorway. Jeremy recognized him. *Oh God, no. I can't take this.*

"Mr. Roberts? I'm Doctor Macklin. We've been looking for you. Please come out in the hallway with me so we can talk."

Jeremy started to go, but Kelly called to him. "Doctor, please. Kaitlin's my sister as well as Jeremy's wife. I want to know what's going on."

"Is that acceptable to you, Mr. Roberts?" he asked. When Jeremy nodded, he said, "All right. One of my colleagues, Doctor Asiphano, will be joining us in a few minutes. He needed a few minutes after operating on your wife. Mr. Roberts, I need to apologize for sending you out so qu—"

"It's okay, Doc," Jeremy interrupted. "I understand."

The doctor frowned. "Your wife's placenta tore from the uterine wall, and an artery ruptured, hence, all the blood you saw. We had to deliver your second child by emergency C-section before we could repair the artery. We immediately gave your wife blood, but she was losing it quicker than we could provide it. We called in a vascular surgeon who was just finishing up another operation. We gave your wife eight units of blood before she left us."

Jeremy thought he could take it, but at the words, 'before she left us,' he started to lose control. His wonderful, perfect Katie was dead.

The room was spinning. Jeremy remembered their first kiss. Asking her for her hand in marriage. Caressing her lips at their wedding. He remembered her laugh, her voice, her delectable scent. *Now she's gone forever.* The room was spinning faster. *Wait for me, Katie. I can't do this without you.*

A second physician entered, concern on his face. "I am Doctor Asiphano. I operated on your wife, Mr. Roberts. She had more issues than we initially thought.

We opened her up so we could stop the arterial bleed in the uterine wall. The entire artery was bulged and about to rupture in several places. We worked on them one by one."

Tears ran down Jeremy's face. He could no longer stand it. "Thank you for everything you tried to do. When did she die?"

The doctors exchanged a strange look before Dr. Macklin answered, "I'm sorry? I thought you knew. Your wife's in recovery. The point I was making is that she was fortunate this happened when it did. Her artery could have ruptured at any time. Let's just be thankful it was here at the hospital."

I've lost my mind. Jeremy backed away. "I'm sorry. W-W-What did you say?"

"Your wife's in recovery."

"She's alive?"

"Yes. Your wife must be special because Someone was watching over her. I'm glad she made it, Mr. Roberts. You can be there when she wakes up. But first, would you like to meet your daughters? They're both healthy."

Jeremy's tears were still flowing, but now, they were tears of happiness. He moved to the bed and hugged Kelly and Geeter, thanking God over and over again for pulling Kaitlin through. "No, thank you, doctor. I want their mother to see them at the same time I do. And doctors... thank you for saving her life. I couldn't have lived another day without her."

***

The world around her rolled in and out of focus as Kaitlin came out of the anesthesia. The first thing she sensed was Jeremy's hand holding hers. Strong, warm, loving. Jeremy was there waiting by her side, like he'd promised. The first thing to come into focus were Jeremy's electric blue eyes smiling back at her. Those eyes were what she had first fallen in love with. The eyes she wanted to see from now to eternity.

Jeremy bent over and kissed her.

It felt so good to have him hold her. When their hug finally ended, she held his hands. "Didn't think I'd ever see your face again."

He shushed her fears with another tender kiss.

The recovery nurse came over to give her ice chips, asking if she wanted juice or soda. Kaitlin laughed. "Better drink a diet soda. Need to lose all the weight I put on during the pregnancy!"

After an hour, they moved her into a room with a familiar roommate. As she was wheeled in, Kelly squealed with delight and waved at her sister. Jeremy pushed her bed close to Kelly's. The sisters held hands as they smiled at each other.

Kelly broke the silence. "Katie, the whole family is here, waiting to see you and your girls."

Her heart filled with joy. *My girls! I'm a mother.* "Kelly, I haven't met them yet." The words were no sooner out of her mouth when a nurse rolled in two tiny plastic bassinets. Kaitlin's chin quivered as she and Jeremy reached for their daughters. Then they took turns passing them back and forth.

Kelly and Geeter were silent as they watched the new family meet and greet each other. Kaitlin couldn't stop saying silent prayers of thanks as she examined her daughters. As she held baby Kelli, she sniffed, then laughed. "Daddy, Kelli has a present for you!" Jeremy also laughed as he reached for his older daughter. He was changing Kelli when the nurse brought in Kelly and Geeter's little girl.

"Aunt Kaitlin, meet your niece, Kaitlin Elizabeth Smith, named in honor of you."

The joy was too much. Kaitlin's face screwed up as she handed Megan to Geeter. She took her niece in her arms. The babies were passed around between mommies, daddies, aunts and uncles. Before long, more aunts, uncles, nieces, nephews, Mimi, and Papaw arrived. Never before had three little ones been welcomed with such love. Three darling girls.

Suddenly a strange man appeared at the door. "I am looking for Kelly Smith. Is she here?"

Kelly smiled. "That's me!"

He frowned. "Sorry to rain on your parade, but here." He handed her an envelope before quickly leaving.

Kelly read it, and her face settled into lines of displeasure. She handed it to Martina.

Martina read it. "Well, it seems the good doctor—and I'm being facetious here—has decided he needed to know right away if baby Kaitlin is his biological child. He had a judge issue an order for a DNA test."

Aunt Kaitlin was upset, but Kelly's voice was full of anger. "Oh, my God, she's not even eight hours old. Does anyone else think that was way too quick! Suppose I don't want my little girl to go through that?" Kelly asked.

Martina shook her head sadly. "I'm afraid you don't really have a choice. This is a court order."

Geeter held Kelly. "It doesn't matter if he's the biological father or not, she's our daughter and to me, she'll always be my little girl. We'll get through this together, no matter what, Sugar-Pie."

***

Kelly wished her time in Chicago wouldn't end so soon. Their house in Chattanooga would be finished in mid-October, and they planned to move the first week of November. The family Thanksgiving gathering would be at their farm in Tennessee.

For the moment, the Jenkins house was almost at capacity with seven children and six adults, but nobody seemed to mind. Cassandra and John were in town as well, but were staying at Martina and Gary's house. A big family get-together was planned for Saturday, but on Friday afternoon, the doorbell rang.

Stan answered the door. He raised his eyebrows when he found both of his eldest daughters and their families standing there. Kelly was a bit confused. She thought they were going out to dinner.

Martina hugged her dad and asked, "May we come in, Daddy?"

"Of course, honey. Where are my manners?"

Kelly had just finished nursing. Baby Katy was warm and heavy as her fingers clung to the blanket. Kelly was walking as she patted her back. Geeter was sitting, David on his lap. Jeremy was helping Kaitlin walk down the stairs after putting their little ones down for a nap. *Thank You, God, for this family.*

Kaitlin said, "Hey, guys! What a pleasant surprise! Wait, I thought you were all going to dinner and then to a ball game tonight."

Martina rarely smiled, but Kelly thought she absolutely glowed. "We were, but something came up that trumped baseball." Her face turned grave, but a hint of a smile tugged at the corners of her mouth. She stared at Kelly. Kelly's hands were suddenly sweaty. "We received the lab results of the DNA test. You'd better sit down."

Oh no. Kelly took a deep breath. Geeter reached over to hold her hand. His strength was always a comfort. "What were they, Martina?"

Her sister pulled an envelope from her pocket, took out her reading glasses, and read aloud. "The results of the DNA testing in comparison to both subjects, Todd Alexander Andrews and baby Kaitlin Elizabeth Smith show..." She paused for dramatic effect. "that these two subjects have a... zero percent probability of being related!"

Kelly jumped to her feet. "So that means—"

Martina interjected, "That means Todd is not her father!"

Geeter jumped to his feet, doing a happy dance as he sang, "She's my daughter! She's my daughter! I knew it!" He grabbed Kelly as she held the baby, smothering her face with kisses. Suddenly, he stopped, his face sober. "...Unless you slept with someone else besides Andrews and me." His eyes dropped to the floor. "S'okay if you did. Did you?"

Kelly was on cloud nine. She laughed and kissed his lips. "Nope, she's yours, honey. All yours!" And then she threw her head back and laughed some more.

"What's so funny?" Geeter asked.

All eyes were glued to Kelly, but she only had eyes for one man. She passed off little Katy to the eager hands of Nora, who'd already been let in on the secret. Then she stood up directly in front of her husband and took both his hands. "It's just that... well... Geeter, you and I are going to be parents again. What do you..."

She never got the chance to finish. Her husband jumped up, lifted her in his arms and swung her around. He started hooting and hollering with joy. "You've made me the happiest man in the world, Sugar Britches! I love you, I love you, I love you!"

As Kelly looked into Geeter's eyes, all she could see reflected back was happiness.

The End

Other Books by this Author

Seeking Forever (Book 1)

Kaitlin Jenkins long ago gave up the notion of ever finding true love, let alone a soulmate. Jeremy is trying to get his life back on track after a bitter divorce and an earlier than planned departure from the military. They have nothing in common, except their distrust of the opposite sex.

An unexpected turn of events sends these two strangers together on a cross-country journey—a trip fraught with loneliness and unexpected danger. And on this strange voyage, they're forced to rely on each other—if they want to survive. But after the past, is it even possible to trust anyone again?

Seeking Forever is the first book of Chas Williamson's Seeking series, the saga of the Jenkins family over three generations.

Will Kaitlin and Jeremy ever be the same after this treacherous journey?

Seeking Happiness (Book 2)

Kelly was floored when her husband of ten years announced he was leaving her for another woman. But she isn't ready to be an old maid. And she soon discovers there's no shortage of men waiting in line.

Every man has his flaws, but sometimes the most glaring ones are well hidden. And now and then, those faults can force other people to the very edge, to become everything they're not. And when that happens to her, there's only one thing that can save Kelly.

Seeking Happiness is the second book of Chas Williamson's Seeking series, the saga of the Jenkins family over three generations.

Ride along with Kelly on one of the wildest adventures you can imagine.

Seeking Eternity (Book 3)
At eighteen, Nora Thomas fell in love with her soulmate and best friend, Stan Jenkins. But Nora was already engaged to a wonderful man, so reluctantly, Nora told Stan they could only be friends. Stan completely disappeared (well, almost), from her world, from her life, from everywhere but Nora's broken heart.

Ten painful years later, the widow and mother of two was waiting tables when she looked up and found Stan sitting in her section. But she was wearing an engagement ring and Stan, a wedding ring. Can a woman survive when her heart is ripped out a second time?

Seeking Eternity is the third book of Chas Williamson's Seeking series, a glimpse at the beginning of the Jenkins' family saga through three generations.

Will Nora overcome all odds to find eternal happiness?

Seeking the Pearl (Book 4)

Eleanor Lucia has lived a sad and somber life, until she travels to London to open a hotel for her Aunt Kaitlin. For that's where Ellie meets Scotsman Henry Campbell and finally discovers true happiness. All that changes when Ellie disappears without a trace and everyone believes she is dead, well almost everyone.

But Henry and Ellie have a special bond, one that defies explanation. As if she were whispering in his ear, Henry can sense Eleanor begging him to save her. And Henry vows he will search for her, he will find her and he will rescue her, or spend his last breath trying.

Seeking the Pearl is the exciting finale of Chas Williamson's Seeking series, the culmination of the three generation Jenkins' family saga.

Henry frantically races against time to rescue Ellie, but will he be too late?

Whispers in Paradise (Book 1)

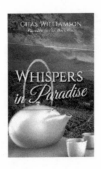

Ashley Campbell never expected to find love, not after what cancer has done to her body. Until Harry Campbell courts her in a fairy tale romance that exceeds even her wildest dreams. But all that changes in an instant when Harry's youngest brother steals a kiss, and Harry walks in on it.

Just when all her hopes and dreams are within reach, Ashley's world crumbles. Life is too painful to remain in Paradise because Harry's memory taunts her constantly.

Yet for a woman who has beaten the odds, defeating cancer not once, but twice, can anything stand in the way of her dreams?

Whispers in Paradise is the first book in Chas Williamson's Paradise series, stories based loosely around the loves and lives of the patrons of Sophie Miller's Essence of Tuscany Tea Room.

Which brother will Ashley choose?

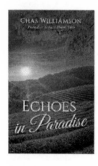

Echoes in Paradise (Book 2)

Hannah Rutledge rips her daughters from their Oklahoma home in the middle of the night to escape a predator from her youth. After months of secrecy and frequent moves to hide her trail, she settles in Paradise and ends up working with Sam Espenshade, twelve years her junior. Sam wins her daughters' hearts, and earns her friendship, but because of her past, can she ever totally trust anyone again?

Yet, for the first time since the death of her husband, Hannah's life is starting to feel normal, and happy, very happy. But a violent attack leaves Sam physically scarred and drives a deep wedge between them. To help heal the wounds, Hannah is forced from her comfort zone and possibly exposes the trail she's tried so hard to cover.

Echoes in Paradise is the second book in Chas Williamson's Paradise series, an exciting love story with Sophie Miller's Essence of Tuscany Tea Room in background.

When the villain's brother shows up on Hannah's doorstep at midnight on Christmas Eve, were the efforts since she left Oklahoma in vain?

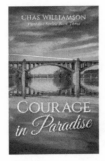

Courage in Paradise (Book 3)

Sportscaster Riley Espenshade returns to southcentral Pennsylvania so she can be close to her family while growing her career. One thing Riley didn't anticipate was falling for hockey's greatest superstar, Mickey Campeau, a rough and tall Canadian who always gets what he wants... and that happens to be Riley. Total bliss seems to be at her fingertips, until she discovers Mickey also loves another girl.

The 'other girl' happens to be Molly, a two-year old orphan suffering from a very rare childhood cancer. Meanwhile, Riley's shining career is rising to its zenith when a new sports network interviews her to be the lead anchor. Just when her dream job falls into her lap, Mickey springs his plan on her, a quick marriage, adopting Molly and setting up house.

Courage in Paradise is Chas Williamson's third book in the Paradise series, chronicling the loves and lives of those who frequent Sophie Miller's Essence of Tuscany Tea Room.

Riley is forced to make a decision, but which one will she choose?

Stranded in Paradise (Book 4)

When Aubrey Stettinger is attacked on a train, a tall, handsome stranger comes to her assistance, but disappears just as quickly. Four months later, Aubrey finds herself recuperating in Paradise at the home of a friend of a friend.

When she realizes the host's brother is the hero from the train, she suspects their reunion is more than a coincidence. Slowly, and for the first time in her life, Aubrey begins to trust—in family, in God and in a man. But just when she's ready to let her guard down, life once again reminds her she can't trust anyone. Caught between two worlds, Aubrey must choose between chasing her fleeting dreams and carving out a new life in this strange place.

Stranded in Paradise is the fourth book in the Paradise series, chronicling the loves and lives of those who frequent Sophie Miller's Essence of Tuscany Tea Room.

Will Aubrey remain *Stranded in Paradise*?

Christmas in Paradise (Book 5)

True love never dies, except when it abandons you at the altar.

Rachel Domitar has found the man of her dreams. The church is filled with friends and family, her hair and dress are perfect, and the honeymoon beckons, but one knock at the door is about to change everything.

Leslie Lapp's life is idyllic – she owns her own business and home, and has many friends – but no one special to share her life... until one dark and stormy afternoon when she's forced off the highway. Will the knock at her door be life changing as well?

When love comes knocking at Christmas, will they have the courage to open the door to paradise?

About the Author

Chas Williamson's lifelong dream was to write. He started writing his first book at age eight, but quit after two paragraphs. Yet some dreams never fade...

It's said one should write what one knows best. That left two choices—the world of environmental health and safety... or romance. Chas and his bride have built a fairytale life of love. At her encouragement, he began writing romance. The characters you'll meet in his books are very real to him, and he hopes they'll become just as real to you.

True Love Lasts Forever!

Follow Chas on
www.bookbub.com/authors/chas-williamson

Enjoyed this book?
Please consider placing a review on Amazon!